texas wind

ALSO BY JAMES REASONER

TEXAS WIND
STARK'S JUSTICE
THE HAWTHORNE LEGACY
THE DIABLO GRANT
WIND RIVER
THUNDER WAGON
WOLF SHADOW
MEDICINE CREEK
DARK TRAIL
JUDGMENT DAY
THE WILDERNESS ROAD
THE HUNTED
UNDER OUTLAW FLAGS

DRAW: THE GREATEST GUNFIGHTS OF THE AMERICAN WEST (Non-fiction)

The Last Good War: (WWII Saga)
    Book 1: BATTLE LINES
    Book 2: TRIAL BY FIRE
    Book 3: ZERO HOUR

Civil War Battle Series: (Family Saga)
    Book 1: MANASSAS
    Book 2: SHILOH
    Book 3: ANTIETAM
    Book 4: CHANCELLORSVILLE
    Book 5: VICKSBURG
    Book 6: GETTYSBURG
    Book 7: CHICKAMAUGA
    Book 8 SHENANDOAH
    Book 9: SAVANNAH
    Book 10: APPOMATTOX

texas wind

james reasoner

introduction by Ed Gorman

POINTBLANK

Set in Sabon

POINT*BLANK* is an imprint of Wildside Press
PO Box 301, Holicong, PA 18928-0301
www.wildsidepress.com
www.pointblankpress.com

edited by Juha Lindroos and Allan Guthrie

For more information contact Wildside Press

ISBN: 1-930997-50-7 (HB)
ISBN: 1-930997-51-5 (PB)

For Livia,
Who was there from the start,
And now for Shayna and Joanna, too

introduction
ed gorman

ONE OF THE nice rewards of writing genre fiction is that some of it lasts for several decades. Right now, for example, there is a revival of certain pulp stories from the Thirties and Forties. And there's a mini-industry in the republication of Fifties and early Sixties paperback originals.

True, you won't find many of these reprints available in most bookstores. Most of them you have to special order from booksellers or order on-line.

With few exceptions, none of the bestsellers of those decades past are being reprinted. Popular as they were, they have vanished.

Pulp fiction owes it's popularity to a relatively small reader base. Open up virtually all of the on-line sites dedicted to pulp and paperback original fiction and you'll find bright, articulate and enthusiastic readers talking about authors who should be brought back into print.

Which brings us to James Reasoner's TEXAS WIND, a novel that went out of print on the same date it was put *into* print. Manor Books, the tiny NYC publishing house that printed it, was crippled with terrible distribution problems. If you found a copy, you were truly blessed.

Readers and fans of TEXAS WIND have kept it alive by discussing it on-line, at conventions and over beers down at the local tap. I've tried to get it back into print a couple of times myself. Finally, it's here.

I've seen it praised for all sorts of reasons, all of them reasonable, all of them true in their way. I'll tell you why I personally find it an important book: because it creates a world, in this case Texas, and fills it out in every way possible—through its characters, its sociology, and perhaps most important of all, the simple decency of its working-class protagonist.

Too much current crime fiction, for my taste anyway, is hyped in the way most TV crime fiction is hyped. Angry cops, slimy villains, sticky sentimental "moments," and endless "crises" that are literally charted out before any actual writing gets done. In sit-coms they use laugh tracks.

In crime dramas they use "moments" so we know that we're getting down and getting gritty. Reality, don't you know. But it isn't reality at all. It's just TV melodrama.

The last crime show I watched with any regularity was "The Rockford Files." A number of critics disliked it because they felt it was "light." I always interpreted this as meaning it had no pretensions. True, it had all the standard car chases and fist fights and tough guy talk. But what they overlooked were all the small, memorable truths. Rockford's melancholy old man. Angel whom you hated yourself for liking. All the quiet sadsack street people that streamed through season after season. Isaac Hayes calling Rockford "Rockfish." The used-up middle-aged ladies Rockford got close to on various occasions. And all the serio-comic con artists who used everything from religion to sex for their larcenous purposes. Remember the white-robed TV minister who spoiled the effect of his ethereal attire by wearing wing-tip shoes?

Quiet, real.

You'll find the same tone and themes in TEXAS WIND. James gives us a real world. People talk about money, their kids, their jobs, getting laid, reading certain books, listening to certain records, watching certain movies. Pop culture references are neatly folded into the action. The stuff real people talk about without breaking into Wagnerian emoting.

Raymond Chandler said that the mystery novel should be so well done that it would satisfy you even if the last chapter was missing. I make that claim for TEXAS WIND and the presentation of its people, rich people, poor people, smart people, dumb people all living inside the hype and hoopla and glorious history of a state every bit as mythic as California itself.

Chandler called THE GREAT GATSBY "a little pure art." Art is in the eye of the beholder and can be argued back and forth until the brewery runs dry.

What can't be argued about is storytelling, the techniques of bedazzling a reader from the opening paragraph and taking him through love, hate, humor, terror, rage and those tiny human moments of reflection and remorse that help us come to grips, however reluctantly, with who we really are in our most secret heart.

What James Reasoner has done is sneak up on us with a piece of first-rate storytelling that will now be in print for many, many years to come.

CHAPTER I

I TOPPED A little rise on Ridgmar Boulevard and could see forever into the west. I could look past Carswell Air Force Base with its giant planes landing and taking off into the brushy hills that rolled gently all the way to Weatherford. It was just past ten o'clock on a Monday morning in October, and the early haze in the air was starting to burn off. The air coming in the window of my Ford had a tang to it that wasn't caused by pollution. The first frost would come before the month was out, I figured.

I almost missed the road where I was supposed to turn. It's a funny thing about the Ridgmar section of Fort Worth. Some of the town's wealthiest people live there, and they'll go to any lengths to make their fancy houses unique, and yet they still all look alike, to me, anyway.

The house I was looking for sat behind a screen of trees and hedges on the side of a hill. An asphalt driveway turned off the road through a gap in the hedge, and I followed it through an acre of lawn. The house at the end of it was a three-way brick with dark wood trim, fairly modest for this neighborhood but still miles above my apartment in Arlington Heights.

I parked in front of the house and slipped my jacket on before I got out of the car. My shirt was clean, and I had brushed up my scuffed boots the best I could. People who lived in places like this probably expected all their employees to be neatly dressed, even private detectives.

The front door was heavy and ornately hand carved. A maid in a black uniform opened it almost as soon as I knocked. She gave me a pleasant but suspicious smile and said, "Yes?"

"My name is Cody," I told her. "I have an appointment with Mrs. Traft."

"Come in, please." I stepped into a hall with a big mirror on one side. "I'll tell Mrs. Traft you're here."

She moved quickly and silently into another room, leaving me in the hall. It was paneled with rich dark wood, making it quite a bit dimmer than the bright sunshine outside. My eyes were just adjusting when I heard footsteps returning. I was facing the mirror, so I stayed that way.

"Mr. Cody? I'm Gloria Traft."

I studied her reflection for a moment before I turned around. She was in the neighborhood of forty, and on her, it was still a very good neighborhood. Her hair was ash blond, her complexion pale. The worried look on her face didn't make it any less attractive. When I turned around, I saw that her eyes were very blue.

"I'm Cody," I nodded. "My service told me you called."

"Please, come into the study."

She wore a powder blue dressing gown that swirled around her feet as I followed her down the hall and into a comfortable room lined with books. She sat down behind a big mahogany desk and motioned at an armchair in front of it. I sat.

"My lawyer recommended you, Mr. Cody," Gloria Traft said. "He wanted to handle this business himself, but I decided I'd feel better taking care of it personally."

She paused as if for me to comment, but I kept my mouth shut. I wanted her to come out with it herself, rather than having to pull it out of her.

After a moment, she went on. "This is about my daughter, Mr. Cody, so discretion is of the utmost importance. My stepdaughter, I should say. I think of Mandy as my own."

I nodded and said, "I understand," even though I didn't, not yet.

She took a deep breath. "I suppose I should be blunt. My stepdaughter Amanda is missing, and I want you to find her, Mr. Cody."

"How long has she been gone?"

"Since last Thursday."

"Have you called the police?"

"No."

Now it was my turn to breathe deeply. "You should. They can look for your daughter a lot better than I can."

She shook her head. "I don't want any publicity. I don't even want this to be a matter of official record."

"Why?" It wouldn't hurt to ask, even if she might not tell me.

"Mandy's father is out of town on business right now. He doesn't know she's missing." Her face twisted just for a second, and I caught a glimpse of the self-control she was imposing on herself. "If you can find Mandy and bring her back before he returns on Wednesday afternoon, he'll never have to know she was gone."

"Are you sure he needs so much protection from the situation?" I couldn't help but ask.

She laced her fingers together on the desk and stared at them. "My husband has a great deal of pressure on him in his business. He doesn't need anything else to worry about."

I thought for a moment and then decided to let that go for now. I said, "Tell me about Mandy."

Mrs. Traft turned a gold-framed picture on the desk around where I could see it. It showed a teenage girl standing on the deck of a sailboat. She wore white shorts and a blue sweater, and her long blond hair was blowing in the wind. She was very pretty.

"This was taken last year," Mrs. Traft said. "She's twenty now, but she hasn't changed much. She's always been a very lovely girl."

"Does she live here with you and your husband?"

"No, she and another girl share a house near the school. Mandy just started her junior year at TCU. She still has a room here, of course."

"And you say she's been gone since Thursday?"

"Yes, she was gone when Lisa got up Thursday morning."

"That's her roommate?"

"Yes. Lisa Montgomery. She and Mandy have been friends for years. They sing together. I mean they have a group, a trio really. A boy named Jeff Willington is the third member."

She wasn't going to volunteer very much. I said, "Mrs. Traft, I'm going to have to know a few things. Do you mind if I just ask you some questions?"

"Not as long as they're relevant."

I had a feeling that her idea of relevant and mine were going to be different. I said, "Was there any trouble between you and Mandy?"

Her blue eyes took on a hard look. She used it on me for a minute and then said, "Why do you ask that? Because I'm her stepmother?"

I sighed. "I'm just trying to find out how the two of you got along. That's the kind of thing I have to know if I'm going to take the job."

"Are you going to take the job?"

I realized I was nodding slowly. "I think I will."

"All right. That means you will keep everything I tell you confidential?"

I nodded again. "If at all possible."

"There was no trouble between Mandy and myself. I suppose we've never been as close as mother and daughter sometimes are, but we've always been friends. We have few interests in common, though."

"How about her father? How do they get along?"

She permitted herself a slight smile. "Mandy is Austin's only child. I know he loves her very much, and I believe she loves him. There was no problem there. They are very close."

"How about friends?"

"Mandy has always been very popular, but as far as close friends go there's no one but Lisa."

"Boyfriends?"

She hesitated. "Mandy and I have never been close enough for me to know more than the basics of her relationships. She has had several boyfriends, but I do not believe any of them were serious. I do know that she just broke up with the most recent one, a boy named Richard Ferrell. He is also a student at TCU."

"Do you know if she was sleeping with him?"

Her eyes got even harder than before. "I suppose that's relevant, too."

"It could be. They could have made up and run off to get married."

"Amanda wouldn't dare. Besides, I think Richard was more interested in her than she ever was in him."

I changed the subject. "What happened when Lisa found out your daughter was gone?"

"She looked around to see if Mandy had left her a note. Mandy's bed had not been slept in, and some of her clothes were gone. Lisa called to see if Mandy had spent the night here, but we had not seen her."

"Why did you wait so long to try to find her? It's been four days."

"I . . . I was hoping that Mandy was just off on some spree, that she would be back in a day or two."

"Has she ever disappeared like this before and then come back on her own?"

"No, never."

"You didn't have much to base that hope on then, did you?" The good mood I had started out with earlier had disappeared with the haze. I didn't wait for Mrs. Traft to answer my question. "Your best bet now would be the police. I can look into it for you, but the cops can do it a lot more efficiently. A trail can get pretty cold in four days."

Her hand went out and plucked a pen from a holder on the desk. She took a check from the middle drawer and began to fill it out. "I told you I do not want the police, Mr. Cody. My lawyer has heard that you are a competent man at this sort of work." She slid the check across the desk. "I'm placing the matter in your hands. Is two thousand dollars satisfactory as a retainer?"

I picked up the check and looked at it, and it looked very nice. I said, "Okay, Mrs. Traft, I'll see what I can find out for you."

I folded the check and put it in an inside pocket, taking out my notebook as I did so. "I'll need the address where Mandy and Lisa live, and also Richard Ferrell and this Jeff Willington."

She gave me the first one from memory and then looked up the other two in a black address book. Ferrell lived in the TCU area, not far from the girls, and Willington had an apartment on Byers, just off Camp Bowie Boulevard, less than two miles from where I lived.

When I had written down the information, I said, "Do you have a picture of Mandy that I can use? I'll return it."

"Yes, I have some snapshots." She looked in another desk drawer, found a photograph and handed it to me. "You can keep it. It was taken at her high school graduation."

Mandy Traft was just as pretty in this picture as in the other one. I slipped it into my shirt pocket and said, "If you don't mind, I'd like to take a look at Mandy's room here."

"Why is that necessary?"

"When you're looking for a missing person, it always helps if you can get some idea of what that person is like."

She frowned and a brief shudder passed through her. I wondered if it was just soaking in on her that Mandy was indeed a missing person.

"All right," she said after a moment. "I'll show you where it is."

I was a little surprised. She could have had the maid show me the room.

We went back out into the hall and up a flight of stairs at the end of it. Mandy's room was on the second floor at the front of the house, and when Mrs. Traft opened the door to it, I saw that a big window overlooked the vast green lawn.

The room was large and bright, the walls painted a pastel blue. A double bed with a sparkling white spread was on one side, a massive wooden dresser on the other. A portable color TV was on a stand at the foot of the bed, and there was a modular stereo unit next to the dresser. A chest with several drawers stood on one corner. There was some make up, a mirror and a hairbrush on top of the dresser, but nothing else. I opened the dresser drawers and looked in them quickly, because Mrs. Traft was frowning her disapproval at me.

I found more make-up, some stationery and a few paperback books in the dresser. The drawers in the chest contained a few sweaters and some lingerie, and in the closet were only two blouses, a pair of blue jeans and a skirt. There was nothing on the walls.

For all of its neat attractiveness, it was one of the most coldly impersonal rooms I had ever been in. It was hard to believe that a teenaged girl had ever lived here.

"She didn't leave much when she moved out, did she?" I asked Mrs. Traft.

"No, she took most of her things with her. This used to be such a lively room. She had posters and pennants on the walls and stuffed animals all over the bed and Muffin standing guard on the chest."

"Muffin?"

"A jade statuette of a dog, a Pekinese, I believe. My husband bought it for her in Hong Kong. She took all of that with her when she left."

"Was there any particular reason she left here and moved in with Lisa Montgomery?"

"Oh, just a desire for independence, I think. Of course, we paid the rent on the house, but being away from us made her feel like she was on her own."

I nodded and took a last quick look around the sterile room. It still didn't tell me anything.

As we walked down the stairs, I said to Mrs. Traft, "What kind of work does your husband do? His name sounds familiar, but I can't quite pin him down."

"He's an executive with Westco. They manufacture oil field equipment. That's why his work takes him all over the world. He's in Canada right now."

"You said he's supposed to be back Wednesday afternoon?"

"Yes." We had reached the front door, and she opened it for me herself. "I imagine you think I should have let him know about Mandy."

I looked into her blue eyes and said, "That's your decision to make. Just like I decided to take this case."

"I hope we were both right."

"So do I."

We stood there awkwardly for a few seconds, and then she said, "Please find Amanda, Mr. Cody. If anything has happened to her . . ." She let it trail off.

"I'll do what I can," I said.

I FOUND A Seven Eleven store not far from the Traft residence and stopped to make a call from the little open phone booth. When it went through, I said, "Lieutenant Franklin, please.'

It took him about ten seconds to come on the line. He said, "Franklin, Records."

"Hello, Tom, this is Cody."

"You want something, right?"

"Only to hear your sweet golden tones."

"Sure, sure. Now what is it? I'm busy."

"Well, since you insist . . . Have you gotten any dead bodies in the last four days that fit this description?" I rattled off Mandy Traft's vital statistics as I watched a kid who looked sixteen pull up to the store in a ten thousand dollar van.

There was a moment's silence as Franklin went through all the DOA reports since last Thursday. Then he said, "Nope, nothing like that. Is she supposed to be a runaway, or a regular missing person, or what?"

"I can't say right now, Tom."

"Okay, it's your skin. You know better than to get involved in active cases, though, Cody."

"Sure. I'm fully grown."

He hung up as the kid came out of the store carrying two six packs of beer. If he was eighteen, then I was a New York sophisticate. But that seems to be the way things work now. Little laws don't matter.

I went back up Ridgmar to the West Freeway and stayed on it until I got to University Drive. I could see the sun reflecting on the mirrored sides of one of the bank buildings in downtown Fort Worth as I exited onto University.

I found the little house that Mandy Traft and Lisa Montgomery shared on a side street just off University, about four blocks from the TCU campus. There were big oaks and elms with thick trunks along the sidewalk. The houses were old and solid looking and close together. Made of brick and stone, some of them even had ivy climbing on the walls. The one I was looking for was built of dark red stone and had a spacious front porch with a swing.

I knew the area was a mixture of college students and older people. The students moved in and then back out quickly; always shifting around, few of them staying a full four years. The other occupants had been here for decades and wouldn't leave until they were dead. I knew they were much more observant than the always hurrying young people. Some of the neighbors might be a good source of information about Mandy Traft.

I found a parking place about half a block away and walked back after I had wedged the Ford between a little red Volkswagen and another one of the growing horde of custom vans. It was the middle of the morning and I didn't know if I'd find Lisa Montgomery at home or not. She might be in a class at this time. There was only one way to find out, though.

I walked up the three steps and onto the porch. I could see lacy white curtains in the front window, and hanging plants decorated three sides of the porch. I rapped my knuckles on the facing of the screen door.

About a minute passed before I saw a slight twitch of movement at the curtains. Then the door opened two inches. A chain lock stopped it. I was sure the screen was hooked, too.

"Yes? Can I help you?"

The voice was young and went well with the brown eyes and dark brown hair. I said, "Lisa Montgomery?"

"Yes?"

"My name is Cody." I held up the little leather folder that contained my driver's license and P.I.'s license and let her study both of them. "I've been hired by Mrs. Traft to locate Mandy. I'd like to talk to you for a few minutes, if you don't mind."

"Oh." She was still hesitant. "I guess it's okay. Just a minute."

She closed the door and took the chain off, then reopened it and, sure enough, unhooked the screen. She pushed it open and said, "Come in.

I stepped inside. The living room was opened up to my left and there was a soap opera playing on a TV set in the far corner. Lisa crossed the room to turn it off.

She was twenty, Mandy's age, and quite pretty, although not classically beautiful like Mandy. Lisa's dark hair was parted in the middle and fell in waves to her shoulders, framing a face that would look very good with an impish grin on it. She wore a beige sweater, a white shirt and blue jeans.

"I'll do anything I can to help, Mr. Cody," she said. "I've been worried sick ever since Mandy disappeared."

I gestured at the sofa. "You mind if I sit down?"

"Oh no. Go right ahead."

I went right ahead, pulling out my notebook as I did so. Lisa sat down in a wooden rocker. The room, with its long sofa, overstuffed armchairs and fragile looking coffee table with a crocheted doily in the center, reminded me of my sister's house in Dallas.

"It would probably be best," I said, "if you just started with last Wednesday night and told me everything that happened."

She nodded. "Do you know about Friendship?"

"What?"

"Friendship. It's the name of our group. Mandy and Jeff and me."

"Jeff Willington, right? Mrs. Traft told me you sang. Professionally?"

"Sometimes. Jeff plays guitar, I play piano, and we all sing. Wednesday was our last night at the Texas Moon."

"The Texas Moon Cafe?"

"Yes."

I knew the place. It was a supper club catering to Fort Worth's well-heeled upper middle class. The atmosphere was strictly ersatz cowboy, exploiting the Cowtown image for all it was worth. I had been there once and hadn't cared for it.

"We had been playing there for two weeks," Lisa went on, "and closed out Wednesday night. Then we came back here. Jeff left pretty soon after we got here, a little after midnight, I guess. He had a class on Thursday morning. I was tired, so I went on to bed. Mandy was still up. When I woke up the next morning, she wasn't there. Her bed looked like it hadn't been slept in. I looked in her closet and some of her clothes were gone. I just figured she'd gone home, even though I didn't know why she would. I called her mother then. She hadn't seen Mandy all week. That's when I started worrying."

"What did you do then?"

"I called everybody we know. None of them had seen Mandy. I called Mrs. Traft back and asked if I should call the police. She said not to."

"How long have you and Mandy known each other?"

"All our lives." Her mouth tightened and I could see the strain in her eyes. "She's my best friend. We grew up on the same street."

"She's never gone off like this before?"

"Never."

I closed my notebook. "Did she seem upset last Wednesday night?"

"No, everything was fine."

"There was no trouble between the two of you."

She shook her head. "No."

"How about between her and this Jeff Willington?"

"There was no trouble between them. We're all good friends."

"How do Mandy and her mother get along?" Lisa might have a truer picture of that relationship than Mrs. Traft did.

"Fine. That word's getting overworked, isn't it? But that's the best way to describe it. They weren't real close, but they didn't fight or anything. Mrs. Traft isn't Mandy's real mother, you know."

"I know. You said you've known Mandy all her life. What happened to her real mother?"

Lisa rocked back and forth for a moment with a faraway look on her face, then said, "She died."

When she didn't say anything else, I asked, "Can you tell me about it?"

She stood up suddenly and went to the window. Looking out at the street, she said, "There's not much to tell. Her mother was sick for a long time and then died. Mandy and I were seven, I believe. We lived across the street from each other. Everyone knew Mrs. Traft was sick. A woman came during the day and stayed with her while Mr. Traft was at work. One day, it was during the summer, we were playing in Mandy's front yard. Her father came home and hurried into the house. I thought it was funny, him being home in the middle of the day. We went on playing, though. I remember Mandy had Ken and I had Barbie. Then Mr. Traft came out and took Mandy inside. She came back out a few minutes later and sat down and picked up Ken. She said, 'Mama just died.' That's all. 'Mama just died.' I never saw her cry."

I sat there quietly for a moment after Lisa stopped talking, trying to think of something appropriate to say. She saved me the trouble by turning around and saying, "But all that happened thirteen years ago. You're not interested in that. Tell me what else I can do to help you find Mandy."

"All right. Tell me more about her. What kind of person she was, what sort of things she liked."

Lisa smiled slightly. "We've always been best friends. When we were little girls, we'd giggle and tell secrets. You know the kinds of things little girls do."

It was my turn to smile. "Not really. It's been a long time since I've known any little girls. All I have is nephews. The two of you have always gotten along well, then?"

"Oh, there were little spats every now and then, when Mandy would try to take one of my toys or something. Nothing major, though."

"Whose idea was it that you share this house?"

"Mandy's. She decided last spring. She wanted to be out more on her own. I thought it was a good idea."

I shifted on the sofa. It was a little too soft to be completely comfortable. "You said you grew up on the same street. How did the Trafts wind up in Ridgmar?"

"After Mandy's mother died, her father seemed to work harder than ever. He just kept going higher and higher in the company he worked for. He married Gloria two years later and they moved two years after that, when Mandy was eleven."

"And Mandy felt no resentment toward her stepmother?"

"Why are you asking about all this?" A suspicious glint had appeared in her eyes. "This is all ancient history. How will it help you find Mandy now?"

I told her the same thing I had told Mrs. Traft earlier. "When you're looking for someone, it always helps to know who you're looking for. If you'd rather not answer, that's all right, though."

She shook her head wearily. "No, I don't mind. I'm sorry I snapped at you. I'm just worried, that's all."

"I understand. Just a few more things, please. What happened after the Trafts moved? I take it you and Mandy stayed close."

"Yes, as much as we could. Both of my parents were killed in a car wreck and I went to live with my grandfather. He died last year, and it wasn't long after that that Mandy came up with the idea of us sharing this house."

"Tell me a little bit about Jeff Willington and this trio you've got."

"We formed it earlier this year. We're all music majors and we would practice together sometimes, and it just kind of evolved. We've had a few jobs. Mandy doesn't need the money, of course, but it sure comes in handy for Jeff and me."

"Are Mandy and Jeff close?"

"They're friends, of course, but . . . well, really, Jeff and I, ah, we're . . ."

"Okay, I get it. You and Jeff are a twosome, not Mandy and Jeff."

She nodded. I went on, "Mrs. Traft mentioned someone named Richard Ferrell. He used to be Mandy's boyfriend, is that right?"

"He thought he was, anyway. They went out a few times, and he hung around here a lot, but I don't think she was ever really interested in him."

"Did he ever spend the night?"

Her face got that suspicious look again, and I said, "I know you think it's none of my business. But I'm going to be talking to Ferrell, and I'd like to know for sure what his status is."

She thought about it for a minute, then said, "He never spent the night. They weren't lovers."

"All right. What else does Mandy do besides go to school and sing?"

Lisa shrugged. "I don't know, the usual things, I suppose. She goes out some with different boys. She likes swimming and skiing. When I lived with my grandfather, she'd come out to his ranch and we'd go horseback riding. She liked that. She likes all kinds of animals."

I put my hands on my knees and stood up. "Do you think I could take a look at her room here?"

Lisa glanced at a clock on the wall. It was a few minutes past eleven. "I've got a class at eleven thirty," she said hesitantly.

"It won't take but a minute."

"Well . . . all right."

We went into the hall. There was a bathroom right in front of us, with a bedroom on each side. Lisa turned towards the one on the right, the one at the front of the house.

She paused in front of the closed door. "I straightened the room up a little bit," she said. "I hope I didn't do anything wrong."

"Was the room messy, like she left in a hurry and didn't care?"

"Oh, no. It wasn't messy. Cleaning it up was just . . . something to do while I worried."

She turned the knob and opened the door, then stood aside to let me enter first.

It was smaller and not as airy as the room in the Traft house, but it had a lot more personality. There were posters of John Denver and Linda Ronstadt on the wall, a pennant from Country Day School and an original abstract painting. I gestured at the swirl of colors and asked, "Did Mandy paint that?"

"Yes. As far as I know, it's her only painting. Pretty good, don't you think?"

"Well . . . I don't know much about art. My tastes run more to Frederick Remington and Charlie Russell."

"I don't think I know their work. What do they paint?"

I hadn't intended to start a discussion on Art Appreciation. I said, "Do you mind if I poke around some?"

"Not if it's to help you find Mandy."

There was no TV in the room, but there was a record player with a stack of records on the floor beside it. I flipped through them, finding a wide assortment of artists, ranging from the Beatles to Willie Nelson.

The bed was a twin size, and it was covered with the stuffed animals that Mrs. Traft had mentioned. I saw a dog, a cat, a chipmunk, a tiger and an aardvark. There were others, but I didn't have the slightest idea what they were.

I knelt beside the bed and raised the fluffy white spread to look underneath it. There was nothing on the floor under the bed but a wadded up tissue and a bobby pin. I dropped the spread and stood up. Lisa was looking at me with a strange expression on her face. I suppose it did look kind of silly, a grown man peeking under beds.

I started to open the drawers in a redwood chest next to the bed, then hesitated and looked at Lisa. "Go ahead," she said.

All I found were clothes. That left a desk that was angled into one corner.

The top of it was bare. I said, "Was Mandy normally that neat?"

"No, I cleaned the things off of it that were on top. They're all in the middle drawer."

I slid it open and saw several envelopes, some pencils and pens, and a framed photograph lying face down. I picked it up and turned it over.

It was a studio shot. I recognized Mandy and Lisa immediately. They were sitting down, and standing behind them was a boy about the same age, with medium-long dark blond hair. All three of them were smiling at the camera.

"Jeff Willington?" I asked.

"Yes, that's a publicity shot for Friendship. Mr. Traft had them made. He said we had to go first class."

I replaced the picture and started sorting through the envelopes. There were a couple of notes to Mandy from her stepmother, an invitation to a party held six months earlier and half a dozen envelopes addressed to Mandy in a cramped scrawling hand. There was no return address on any of them.

I arranged them according to the dates they were postmarked, then pulled a single sheet of paper from the first one. The handwriting on it was the same as on the envelopes. It began, "Dearest darling Mandy . . ."

I glanced down at the bottom of the sheet. Sure enough, it was signed, "Your ever-faithful Richard." Between that opening and closing were several paragraphs of flowery protestations of love. I didn't know kids wrote such stuff anymore.

The other letters were all in the same vein. The dates on the envelopes ranged from three months earlier to just two weeks before Mandy disappeared. I said, "It looks like this guy Ferrell was devoted to Mandy."

"He was like a puppy," Lisa said. "I don't think she ever really felt anything for him, though."

"Did she let him think she did?"

"I never said Mandy was perfect, Mr. Cody."

I put the letters back on the desk and went through the other drawers. There was nothing unusual in them. School books, sheet music, stationery, things like that. No diary. That was a disappointment.

"All right," I said, "that leaves the closet. Some of Mandy's clothes were gone, right?"

"Yes. Look, Mr. Cody, I'm going to be late for class—"

"This won't take long." I opened the door to the closet and poked through it rapidly, finding a lot of shoes and blue jeans, but nothing out of the ordinary. "Could you tell me which clothes are missing?"

"Let's see . . . There was a green blouse and a blue shirt and a red shirt and two pairs of jeans and some deck shoes and her brown loafers."

"Nothing dressy?"

"No. Just comfortable clothes. Does that mean anything?"

"It could. It could mean she was planning on doing quite a bit of traveling and that she knew she wouldn't be going anywhere fancy."

"You think she ran away on her own?"

"I don't know. I don't have enough information to say anything for sure yet. But a lot of people do it, more than you'd ever think."

"A person would have to be awfully unhappy to run away like that."

"Maybe Mandy covered it up."

Lisa shook her head. "I don't think so."

I closed the closet door. Lisa said, "What will you do now?"

"Talk to some more people. That's about all I can do until I turn up something concrete. I'll have to talk to Jeff Willington and Richard Ferrell. I'll ask the neighbors if they saw anything unusual late Wednesday night or early Thursday morning. I've already checked with the police for unidentified bodies."

I said it without thinking. Lisa turned very pale, gave a little shudder and walked out of the room in a hurry.

I followed and started to apologize when she said, "I've really got to get to class, Mr. Cody. I hope you find Mandy." It was a dismissal, there was no doubt about that.

"Thank you for your help, Miss Montgomery," I said. I let myself out the front door and went down the walk, fallen leaves crackling under my boots.

I had just gotten into my car when the door of the house opened again and Lisa came out, carrying her purse and a notebook. She locked the door behind her. She turned onto the sidewalk and hurried away in the opposite direction from where I was parked. I reached up and twisted the rear view mirror so that I could see her reflection moving away from me.

I was watching Lisa and almost didn't notice that someone was watching me. An instinct that had developed over the years picked up the tiny pressure of eyes on me, though, and I shot a glance across the street.

A boy was sitting in an old Dodge Dart parked diagonally across the street from me. He had a newspaper, and when he saw me looking at him, he tried to raise it and look at it casually. He was about as casual as a kid in a graveyard at midnight.

I wondered who he was. He had a broad, pudgy face, and his brown hair curled tightly against his head. I knew he wasn't Jeff Willington. I hadn't seen a picture of Richard Ferrell, but I had a feeling that I might be looking at him now. I wouldn't forget the face or the car. If he was following me, I could always confront him later. I decided not to worry about him for the moment.

I looked back at the rear view mirror. Lisa was three blocks away by now, walking hurriedly so as to get to her class on time. According to my watch, it was 11:28.

A flicker of movement in the mirror attracted my eye. I watched closely as a man stepped out from behind a tree and put a hand on Lisa's arm, stopping her. They were too far away for me to tell much about him, and passing students kept coming between us. I knew it was Lisa only by the clothes she was wearing.

He seemed to be talking excitedly. I saw Lisa shake her head violently, then shrug out of his grip. She said something and turned to walk away.

The man reached out as if to grab her arm again, then thought better of it and let her go. He watched her walk away.

I started the car and pulled away from the curb. By the time I found a driveway to turn around in and got back up the street, the man was gone. I caught just a glimpse of Lisa going into one of the classroom buildings.

I went back and parked the Ford in the same place. The boy in the Dodge Dart who had been watching me was gone, but I would have bet money that he was still lurking in the neighborhood somewhere.

I spent the next hour in the neighborhood myself, going from door to door along the street and asking everyone who was home about Mandy and whether they had seen her leave.

Everyone I talked to seemed to think highly of both Mandy and Lisa, but no one had seen Mandy leave on Wednesday night or Thursday morning. The older people liked the girls because they didn't play loud music or have wild parties. They seemed to be sort of the adopted daughters of the neighborhood.

By twelve thirty, I was ready to concede that I wasn't going to find anything helpful here. I decided the best thing to do next would be to pay a visit to Jeff Willington. Besides, I was hungry, and his apartment wasn't too far from a good pizza place I knew.

I headed back down University toward the freeway, and I hadn't gone a mile before I spotted the battered old Dodge Dart two cars behind.

I didn't try to lose it. I liked knowing that whoever it was would be back there when I wanted him.

CHAPTER II

THE APARTMENT COMPLEX where Jeff Willington lived had seen better days, but it was still a nice enough place. There were tricycles in the courtyard, so at least it wasn't a den of hungry singles. I found an empty parking space and left the Ford there.

The number of Willington's apartment was 27, putting it on the second floor. I walked past a laundry room and a Coke machine and went up a flight of iron stairs in the middle of the complex.

Apartment 27 was down at the far end. I walked along the balcony past doors that didn't quite fit their frames all the way around, allowing the sounds of soap operas and game shows and crying babies to seep out.

The windows in the apartments were small and high. The ones in Number 27 had thick curtains closed behind them. No sounds came from within. I knocked sharply on the door.

There was no answer, so I knocked again after a moment. When there was still no response, I reached down and tried the knob. It was locked. I probably could've gotten past it, but I wasn't going to try to in the middle of a bright October day.

I went back to the car and headed for that pizza. My stomach was rumbling.

The restaurant was between Jeff's apartment and the place where I lived. The atmosphere inside the unpretentious building was quiet and dark. The pizza was always good, the dark beer excellent, and I dreaded the day that the general public discovered just how nice a place it was.

I went inside the building and grabbed an empty booth, waving at Jerry, the proprietor and chief cook. He called out, "Hi Cody! How ya doin'?"

"Fine."

A waitress came up and I ordered a medium pepperoni and a big mug of dark. She brought the beer and I settled back to wait for the pizza and reflect on my morning's work for Gloria Traft.

So far I hadn't accomplished much other than getting a vague picture of Mandy Traft and who she was. My visit to Lisa and the other neighbors hadn't produced any evidence of foul play, or any evidence of any kind, for that matter. It looked as if Mandy had left on her own, headed for who-knows-where.

I still wanted to talk to Jeff Willington, though, and a visit to the Texas Moon Cafe would also be in order. Someone there might be able to shed some light on Mandy's state of mind last Wednesday night.

Then there was the matter of the kid following me. If he was indeed Richard Ferrell, there could be two different reasons for his presence. He could be tagging along because he was worried about Mandy and wanted to be there if I found her, or he could have something to do with her disappearance and wanted to be sure that I *didn't* find her.

I had just started to wonder who the guy was that had accosted Lisa on her way to class when the pizza came, and for a while, I devoted my energies to that.

Jerry came over while I was eating and said, "Hello, Cody. You working?"

"Yeah," I said, around a mouthful of pepperoni and cheese.

"Big case?"

"There's a girl missing and I'm trying to find her."

"Kidnapped by gangsters? Blackmailed, maybe?"

I swallowed the bite of pizza. "Jerry, I keep telling you. Just because I'm a private detective, that doesn't mean I'm Sam Spade or Mike Hammer. It's a job, just like cooking pizza's a job."

He gave me a big knowing grin. "Sure, Cody, whatever you say."

I did the only thing I could to get him off the subject. I asked him, "Say, do you think the Cowboys will beat the Redskins next Sunday?"

That was all it took. We talked football while I finished my pizza and beer, and then I excused myself. There was a phone just inside the door. I flipped through the directory hanging underneath it and found a listing for Jeff Willington. The address matched up. I dropped a quarter in the slot and punched the digits.

I let the phone on the other end burr twenty times before I hung up. I wished I had thought to ask Lisa about his class schedule.

I paid for the meal and waved at Jerry as I walked out. He made a gun out of his hand and fired it at me, slamming down the thumb.

The parking lot in front of the restaurant was fairly full, but not so full that I didn't spot the Dodge Dart lurking between an El Dorado and a New Yorker. It was not the most inconspicuous place to hide.

I gave a mental shrug and got in my own car. I wasn't quite ready to challenge my tail.

The Texas Moon Cafe was on White Settlement Road, along the stretch where the houses are large and expensive. It took me about fifteen minutes to get there. I didn't know if I would find anyone there at this time of the afternoon, but I thought it was worth a try.

The place had been a private residence itself once. It was a sprawling brick building, and I remembered from my one visit that several walls had been knocked out to make one big main room. The decor ran to plastic longhorns on the walls, spittoons that were of course never used, artificial cactus and Remington prints. The pictures were the only things I had liked.

When I pulled up in front, I saw that someone was there, all right, even though it looked like the place wasn't open for business. Pickups and work vans were parked all around, and workmen were scurrying in and out of the place, carrying tools and equipment.

I got out and looked for somebody in charge. The heavy wooden front door was open, so I ambled through it. A beefy man in a white shirt with a cigar in his mouth said, "You looking for somebody, pal?"

"Is the manager around?"

"I'm bossin' this crew."

"No, I mean the manager of the club."

"Yeah, I think he's here." He used the cigar to point at the door across the room. "Go through there. The office is at the end of the hall."

"Thanks. What are they doing to the place, anyway?"

"Remodeling. They're gonna make a disco out of the joint."

I didn't know whether that was a step up or down. Somehow, I couldn't imagine anyone boogying or getting down in a room full of Remington prints. Plastic longhorns, yes.

The office at the end of the hall had PRIVATE on the door. I knocked on it, and a man called, "Come in."

I swung the door open and stepped into the little office. It must have been a storage room when the place was a residence, because it was too small for anything else.

The man at the desk inside looked up at me and said, "Yes? Can I help you?"

The accent was from somewhere up north. He was about forty-five, with a narrow face and sleek dark hair going just slightly gray. His blue suit was expensive. He reminded me a little bit of somebody, but I couldn't say who.

"Are you the manager?" I asked.

He smiled and stood up. "I'm Barney Wilcox. I own the place, run it and occasionally sweep out." He put out a hand.

"My name's Cody." I returned the handshake.

"And what can I do for you, Mr. Cody?"

"I'm a private detective."

The smile stayed on his lips, but his eyes got wary. "Oh? Has there been a complaint about the club?"

"Nothing like that. It has to do with the trio that was playing here last week."

"Friendship?" He frowned slightly, sitting down and waving me into the chair on the other side of the desk. "What about them? They're not in any trouble, are they? I always thought they were nice kids."

"They're not in any trouble as far as I'm concerned. I'm just trying to locate one of them, Mandy Traft. Do you know how I could get in touch with her?"

The frown went away. "Oh, is that all? I've got her address and phone number here somewhere . . ."

He started to rummage around on the cluttered desk. I said, "That's okay. I've already talked to Lisa Montgomery. She doesn't seem to know where Mandy is. No one seems to know."

"You mean she's disappeared?"

"It looks like it. No one's seen her since last Wednesday night."

Wilcox's frown had come back. He sounded genuinely concerned as he said, "That was the night they closed here. The last night before we closed for remodeling, in fact. You say no one's seen her since then?"

"No. Did you notice anything out of the ordinary that night?"

Wilcox shrugged and spread his hands. "Not a thing."

"None of them seemed to be upset?"

"Not that I could tell. I thought they did a good job, just like always. They did a set at eight and then another one at ten. After that, I gave them their checks and they left."

"Do you know if the group has an agent or business manager, some-body like that?"

"I don't think so. I always just paid them personally."

"Had they worked here before?"

"Oh, yeah, several times. I knew the Trafts. They used to come in here fairly often, and it was Mr. Traft who told me about Mandy and her friends."

"You said the Trafts *used* to come here. Don't they anymore?"

He just shook his head and said, "I think Mr. Traft has been traveling a lot in his business. They don't have as much time as they used to."

"But you did hire the group because of them?"

"Don't get me wrong, Mr. Cody. Those kids have talent. Otherwise, they wouldn't have worked here, no matter who their parents were."

"Okay." He seemed to be friendly and interested in the group and was obviously willing to answer what questions he could. I decided to ask a few more. "Mr. Wilcox, did you ever notice, either while the kids were working or at any other time, any friction between them?"

He thought for a moment, then said, "I don't remember any. They always seemed to get along with each other real well. They were good friends. Of course, at times . . ." He hesitated, then stopped, shaking his head.

I waited a moment, then prodded. "At times what, Mr. Wilcox?"

"Well . . . sometimes I got the feeling that there was something go-ing on between Mandy and Jeff Willington. Come to think of it, last Wednesday night I saw the two of them in the hall right after the last show, and there was definitely something going on then."

That didn't agree with what Lisa had told me. "What were they do-ing?"

"They had their heads together, and he was talking real fast, like he was trying to convince her of something. At first I thought they were arguing, but then he kissed her, and believe me, there was no argument between those two."

He grinned at me, but I didn't feel like returning it. His story went directly against what Lisa had told me about her and Jeff being romanti-cally involved. I suddenly wondered if it had been Jeff I had seen talking to Lisa.

I nodded and said, "Thanks. That might help. Do you have a phone I could use?"

He turned the one on his desk around and pushed it toward me. "Help yourself," he said, then started to rise. "Unless it's private . . ."

"No, that's all right. Thank you."

I dialed Jeff Willington's number again, and again I counted twenty futile rings. I cradled the receiver and stood up.

"Thanks for your help," I said to Wilcox, "and for the use of the phone."

"Sure thing. I just wish I had been able to tell you more. Say, would you mind letting me know when you find Mandy? I'm afraid I'll worry about the kid, now that I know she's missing."

"All right." I had started to turn and leave the office when I got curious about something completely irrelevant. "One more thing. Why are you making this place into a disco?"

He bounded up from behind the desk with a grin. "Money, Mr. Cody," he said. "Why else? The Texas Moon Cafe made money. The Texas Moon Disco will make a lot more."

He put a hand on my shoulder and I found myself trapped. "Let me show you around," he bubbled on. "I'm really proud of all the changes we're making."

He led me out into the main room, waving his arms grandly. "We're putting in a lighted dance floor with a computer controlled lighting system. It'll be the most advanced unit in the Metroplex." He pointed at a half completed platform on one side of the room. "A stand for the DJ, of course, and the best speaker system in town."

"Doesn't all this cost a lot of money?"

"You have to spend money to make money, Mr. Cody, as the sages say. It's really something, isn't it?"

It was something, all right, but after the way he had been so cooperative, I wasn't going to tell him what I really thought about it.

I pointed at the artificial cactus and longhorns and said, "Are you going to keep the fixtures?"

"Yeah, I think so. Except the paintings. They just don't fit in."

As if to support his words, a workman walked by carrying a bundle of half a dozen prints in varying sizes. "What are you going to do with them?" I asked.

"I don't know. Haven't really decided yet. I hate to just throw them away."

"Mr. Wilcox," I said, "I think I know somebody who might be interested in taking them off your hands."

Ten minutes later, with my checkbook over a hundred dollars lighter and my arms full of the prints, I went back out to my car. It would have been nice to have the real things, but I didn't think I could quite afford to buy them from the Amon Carter Museum of Western Art.

I stored the prints in the back seat and was about to get in myself when a little red Porsche pulled up behind me. A red-haired woman in a green pantsuit got out and said, "Hello, Mr. Cody."

I looked up and saw a familiar face. "Hello, Mrs. Bryant," I replied.

She stepped up beside my car and looked into the back seat. "I see you still like Remington."

"I like the way he paints. And his subjects."

"I was wondering what Barney was going to do with them."

I had always felt vaguely embarrassed by Janice Bryant. She was the kind of cool redhead who epitomized style and class. She would never see thirty again, but then she didn't need to. I had never been able to understand what she saw in me that prompted her interest.

"I haven't seen you at the museum lately," she went on.

"I've been pretty busy."

Janice was a widow whose husband had died young, leaving her fairly well off. She served as a volunteer docent at the Amon Carter, and since I visited it often to look at the paintings and sculpture, a friendship had developed between us. I had considered trying to turn it into more than a friendship.

"What are you doing here?" I asked, without thinking about how it sounded. Being around her usually got me a little rattled.

"I work here now," she said sweetly. "You're looking at Barney Wilcox's new personal assistant."

I was surprised. I knew her husband had left her some money when he died, but with payments on big fancy houses and little fancy cars, it might not have been enough. I remembered to answer her question.

"No, I don't much care for them."

"That's too bad. Maybe you'll come to see us, anyway."

She turned and started to walk away, toward the club entrance. I never knew whether she was serious or slipping me a needle. I called after her on impulse.

"Janice!"

She turned back, and I thought the smile on her lips was genuine. "Yes?"

"Would you like to have dinner with me tonight?"

She paused thoughtfully. "I think I'd like that," she said. "You know where I live, don't you?"

"Sure. Is seven thirty all right?"

"Excellent. I'll see you then, Mr. Cody."

I watched her go on into the Texas Moon. I wondered if the grin on my face was as silly as those on the workmen who were watching her, too.

I shook my head at my own behavior, scratched an ear and got into my car. It was time I went back to work.

I decided to return to Jeff Willington's apartment. If he still hadn't arrived by the time I got there, I could try talking to the neighbors, maybe get an idea of when he would be there.

I parked the car and went up the metal stairs again. The same sounds were still coming from behind the poorly fitting doors, and the curtains were still pulled at Number 27. I rapped on the door, hard and demanding this time.

I waited a minute, knocked again, then reached down and rattled the knob. There was no response inside.

There was only one more apartment past Willington's. I walked over to the door and paused for a second before knocking on it. I could hear country music coming from a radio inside. The curtains on the window were halfway open.

I knocked on the door, and a second later, the volume on the radio was turned down. The ever-present chain lock let the door open a few inches, and a broad, freckled, female face looked out at me. The woman smiled and said, "Hi!"

I said, "Hi, yourself. You know when Jeff's going to be back?" I gestured next door with a thumb.

She shook her head. She had short blond hair, and I judged her age to be early twenties. She said, "Sorry, I don't have any idea. We just moved here a few weeks ago, and I don't know the neighbors too well. Is there anything else I can help you with?"

"No, I just need to talk to him. You don't know when he usually comes in?"

"I'm afraid not. My husband works all day, and I just stay in the apartment. I could tell Mr. Willington you were here, though, next time I see him. My name's Becky Roberts."

She had her blue eyes wide open and staring at me. I started to say, "No, that's all right," when she suddenly said, "Just a minute." She closed the door, took the chain off and opened it again.

She was wearing a man's work shirt that had trouble coping with her ample figure and blue jeans cut off short to reveal solid, well-shaped legs. She said, "You can come in and wait for him if you want."

She wasn't trying too hard to hide what she had in mind. It must've been pretty boring for her to stay at home in that little apartment all day while her husband was out working.

I smiled and shook my head. "No thanks. Maybe I'll catch him later."

She shrugged. "Okay. No telling when he'll be home, though."

"Thanks anyway."

She shut the door with a sigh and I went back down the balcony, shaking my head.

The apartment on the other side of Jeff Willington's had the sound of a soap opera coming from it. I listened to it for a second until the organ music welled up and a commercial came on.

The woman who answered my knock this time was a direct contrast to Becky Roberts. She was small, dark, middle-aged and wasn't just about to open her door to me or any other strange man. She cracked the door about an inch and said sharply, "Yes?"

"Excuse me," I said, "but do you know when Mr. Willington next door will be home?"

"No, I don't. It's bad enough I have to live next to that hippie. I don't keep up with his hours."

I hadn't heard anyone described as a hippie in a long time. In the picture I had seen of him, Jeff hadn't looked like the type to prompt such a description. A little arrogant and too self-assured, maybe, but still fairly clean cut.

I decided a more authoritarian approach might work better with this woman. I said, "I'm a detective—"

"I don't know anything about it," she cut in. "I'm just a poor widow woman. What he smokes over there is none of my business. I admit I complained to the manager about it, but the smoke was coming through the walls and making me sick. I don't want to be involved with the police, though."

If she was going to leave the ball lying on the ground, I was going to pick it up and run with it. "I think we'll be able to keep your name out of the investigation, ma'am, but we still need to talk to Mr. Willington. He's not home now. Do you have any idea when he might be back?"

"I told you, I don't keep up with his hours. Why, I haven't even seen him in several days."

That little bit of information was much more interesting than the fact that Jeff Willington maybe smoked marijuana. I said, "Do you remember the last time you did see him?"

The narrow strip of face that I could see frowned. "I believe it was last week sometime. Yes, I think it was last Wednesday."

"And you haven't seen him since?"

"No."

"You didn't wonder where he was?"

She snorted. "I don't care where he is. He may have gotten his brain so addled that he's forgotten where he lives. I wouldn't be a bit surprised."

I nodded and said, "Thank you. Sorry to have bothered—"

She shut the door before I could finish my sentence.

I chewed on what she had given me as I walked back down the stairs and into the courtyard. The door of the apartment next to the laundry room bore a sign that read MANAGER. I rapped my knuckles on it.

There was no chain lock this time. A large, raw-boned woman swung the door open and said, "Yeah? Can I help you?"

Her brown eyes had a blunt, honest look to them. I said, "My name is Cody. I'm looking for Jeff Willington, Apartment 27."

"Up on the second floor." She pointed.

"I know; I've been up there already. He's not home."

"Did Mrs. Lansing call the cops on him again? You look like a cop."

She made it a simple statement of fact. I said, "I'm a private investigator. Mrs. Lansing is in Number 26, right?"

"Right. She's always got something to complain about. What did Jeff do wrong?"

"Nothing, as far as I know. I'm really looking for a friend of his, and I thought maybe he could help me. Do you know a girl named Amanda Traft?"

She frowned. "There's a couple of girls I've seen with him, a blonde and a brunette. Would she be one of them?"

"The blonde. Was she here very often?"

"Quite a bit here lately. I used to see the three of them together, but for a while now, the blonde's been coming here by herself. She's the one you're looking for, right?"

"Yes. She's been missing since last Thursday. Mrs. Lansing said she hadn't seen Jeff Willington since last Wednesday. Have you?"

The woman frowned again. "Let me think a minute. No, come to think of it, I don't believe I have. Course, there's so much to keep up with around here that I'm not sure."

"Okay, thanks. I don't suppose you'd let me into his apartment so that I could look around?"

She grinned. "You suppose right, mister. You come back with a real cop and I might, but that's the only way. The company that owns this place wouldn't like it if I let just anybody in, even private eyes. And my husband and I couldn't afford a place like this if we had to pay for it."

I grinned back and said, "Well, I tried."

The woman stopped me by saying, "You think Jeff and that blonde ran off together?"

"It's a possibility." I hoped I didn't sound as grim as I was starting to feel.

"Damn, I hope you find them, then."

"Why's that?"

"Rent's due this Friday."

I could feel the beginnings of anger and frustration inside me as I drove away. In a good percentage of missing person cases, the person is missing of his or her own free will. They leave because of anger or boredom or loneliness, or just because they don't want to be where they are anymore. What do you do when you locate such a person? Drag them back kicking and screaming? Not me, thank you.

For now I'd just keep looking, but if it turned out that Mandy and Jeff had run off together, to get married or whatever, then Mrs. Traft would get that information from me and nothing more. She could hire somebody else for the dragging back part.

I glanced in the rear view mirror and saw, three cars back, the familiar dark blue fender of the Dodge Dart that had been following me all day. I decided that it was time I had a talk with whoever was driving it, especially if it was Richard Ferrell.

I was on Camp Bowie Boulevard. I accelerated a little, just enough to pull away from the traffic around me. The Dodge Dart took the bait, speeding up and closing the gap between us just slightly. I had him hooked.

I had to slow down so that the light where Camp Bowie, Bailey, University, and Sixth and Seventh Streets came together would catch both of us. The Dodge Dart pulled up right behind me, and I could see in the mirror that the driver was staring out his window, pretending not to pay any attention to me.

The wait at the light was always a long one, and this time was no different. When it finally changed to green, I sped away down Seventh Street, past Montgomery Wards, toward downtown Fort Worth. The Dodge Dart dropped back a little bit, into a more circumspect position.

There was a long stretch of warehouses on the right. Without signaling, I whipped into a side street unexpectedly, taking the driver of the Dodge Dart by surprise. He stuck with me, executing the turn rather sloppily.

We were surrounded by loading docks and alleys. The Ford bumped over some railroad tracks, and then I pulled into an alley and stepped on the gas, zooming past broken bottles and cardboard cartons. I exited at the far end of the alley just as the Dodge Dart was starting into it.

He must've been puzzled when he pulled out of the alley and didn't see me anymore. He cruised along the street slowly and finally spotted the Ford parked at the end of a blind alley that dead-ended into a concrete wall. The Dodge Dart came to a stop and he sat there for a long moment, staring down the alley at my car. After hesitating, he got out of his car, leaving the motor running, and began to walk slowly and cautiously down the alley.

I stood up from behind one of the massive tires of an empty eighteen wheeler parked just beyond the alley. I had just about gotten my breath back after parking the car and sprinting back out. I had ducked behind the tire just as the Dodge Dart came out of the other alley.

Now, I stepped into the mouth of the alley and saw the driver of the Dodge Dart bending over and peering into my empty Ford. There was nothing but blank walls around, and he had to be wondering where I had disappeared.

"Looking for somebody?" I asked.

His head jerked around. The expression on his face was desperate. I could see panic in his wide eyes. He was a big man, and he started at me in a lumbering run that turned into the headlong plunge of a locomotive.

I let him get nearly to me before I stepped aside. He tried to slow down, but I reached out and grabbed his shirt, giving him an extra impetus in the direction he was going. That extra push was enough to send him out of control, and he went spinning and crashing into the side of the Dodge Dart.

He bounced off and went to one knee. I stepped in as he struggled to get up, grabbing his shoulders and slamming him back against the car. He cried, "W-wait!"

I backed off as he caught his breath. "Who the hell are you?" I asked. "You've been following me all day, and I don't like it."

He glared at me as he leaned on the car. "I want to know who the hell *you* are! What have you got to do with Mandy Traft? Do you know where she is? Is she all right?"

"Slow down. I don't know where Mandy Traft is. Are you Richard Ferrell?"

"Yeah. Why were you at her house?"

"I was hired by Mandy's mother to find her. My name's Cody."

"You're a private detective?"

"That's right. And if you're so worried about Mandy, the best thing for you to do is answer my questions, not tag along after me. My God, did you even eat any lunch?"

He shook his head. "I didn't think about it. I was too worried. I want to know where Mandy is." His nostrils flared and he started breathing heavily again.

"Now just take it easy," I said quickly. He was four or five inches taller than me and about fifty pounds heavier. "I want to find Mandy just as much as you do. There's no reason why we can't cooperate and help each other."

His look was baleful, but he said, "Well, all right. I guess it won't hurt to talk to you."

"That's better. Now, why have you been following me all day?"

"I saw you talking to Lisa. I thought you might know where Mandy is. I hoped you'd lead me to her."

"Who did you think I was?"

"I didn't know. But I've been watching the house since Thursday, and you're the first stranger who's been there. When you stayed inside so long talking to Lisa, I knew it had to be about Mandy."

"You were right about that."

"When you went to the Texas Moon and to Willington's apartment, I was sure of it."

He seemed to be calmer now. I asked, "How much do you know about Willington?"

"I don't like him," Ferrell replied with a scowl. "He's good looking and he knows it. He's too sure of himself."

"How does Mandy feel about him?"

"What do you mean by that?" He was heating up again. He seemed to have a low boiling point.

I ignored both his question and the fact that he hadn't answered mine. "When did you talk to Mandy last?" I said.

"It was Wednesday afternoon. I asked her if I could see her when she got through at the club that night, and she said no. She said she had something important to do, but she wouldn't tell me what it was."

It looked like running off with Jeff Willington had been a planned thing, rather than a spur of the moment deal. If Barney Wilcox and the manager at the apartments had told me the truth, the relationship had been going on a while, too. I wanted to know why Lisa Montgomery had told me the exact opposite, that Jeff Willington was her boyfriend.

"What have you found out, Mr. Cody?" Ferrell asked. "Do you know where Mandy might be? If something has happened to her, I—I don't think I could stand it!"

The hangdog expression on his face looked ludicrous, but all of a sudden I could sympathize with him. He may have been a big bear on the outside, but on the inside he was just a love-struck kid. Mandy Traft was his golden girl, and I didn't know if I wanted to tarnish the image by telling him that it looked like she had run off with another man.

"Look, Richard," I said, "I don't know where Mandy is, but given time, I'm sure I can find her. I think she's probably all right, and I don't think you should worry."

"What are you going to do?"

"Right now, I'm going back to ask Lisa Montgomery a few more questions. After that, I'm not sure. But the best thing for you to do would be to go home and try to relax. You can give me your phone number, and I'll call you if I find out anything."

He thought it over, then said, "All right. If you promise to call as soon as you know something."

"I promise."

I wrote his number down in my notebook. He squeezed his big body back into the still running Dodge Dart. Before he could put it in gear, I said, "How did Mandy seem last Wednesday, Richard? Was she mad or upset?"

His wide brow wrinkled in a frown. "No, she was excited about something. A little nervous, maybe, but still happy. I wish she'd let me see her that night. Maybe then she wouldn't be gone." He looked up at me. "You will find her, won't you?"

"I'll sure try."

I FOLLOWED A slow moving pickup back toward the TCU campus. A sticker on its rear bumper proclaimed COWGIRLS NEED LOVE TOO!

A lot of classes must've just been letting out because the sidewalks around the school were packed with students. I had to slow down to let some of them cross the street in front of me.

I turned off at University onto the side street where Lisa Montgomery lived. The closest parking place was a little further down the block this time. I maneuvered into it and left the car there.

The house was unchanged since that morning. I knocked on the door several times without getting an answer. The screen door was unhooked, so I opened it and tried the knob. It was locked.

There was a metal lawn chair on the porch by the front window. I sat down in it, ducked my head to keep from hitting a hanging plant and settled down to wait. As I did, I watched the college kids walking by on the sidewalk.

It was only twenty years or so since I was their age, but I couldn't remember ever being that young. I knew better than to think they were all happy and carefree, though. Maybe the problems of youth didn't seem quite so important as you got older, but that didn't mean they were less than earth shaking for the people going through them. Everybody's problems are important at the time.

When I was their age, my main worries were finding a career and finding girls, not necessarily in that order. Now I had a career of sorts and there had been a few women in my life. Being around someone like Janice Bryant still made me feel awkward and slightly embarrassed, though.

That reminded me I had a dinner date later on. I hoped I was in a better mood by then.

I sat there for fifteen minutes, until I spotted Lisa coming down the street. She was carrying several books, and she noticed me about the same time I saw her.

She paused just for a second and then came on, turning onto the walk that led up to the porch. I stood up to meet her.

There was an anxious expression on her face as she said, "Hello, Mr. Cody. Has something happened? Have you found Mandy?"

"Not yet," I said. "Could we go inside and talk?"

"Sure." She opened the screen door as she dug her keys out of her purse. When she had the door unlocked, I followed her into the living room. She put her books down on the TV set.

Turning back to me, she said, "Was there something else you needed to ask me?"

"Yes. Why didn't you tell me Mandy and Jeff were in love?"

She took it better than I expected she would. There was only a momentary flinch, a brief trembling of her lower lip. Then she said, "What are you talking about?"

"You told me that if there was any romance going on in Friendship, it was between you and Jeff. That's not true, is it?"

"Of course it is. Jeff and I even talked about getting married."

"When did you talk about it? Recently?"

"Well, it's been a while . . ."

"Nothing said about it lately?"

"No, but that doesn't mean . . ."

"Mandy's been paying visits to Jeff's apartment by herself, did you know that?"

"All right!" Her voice broke and her hands knotted into fists at her side. "Jeff isn't paying as much attention to me as he used to. Mandy has been acting a little funny. But that doesn't mean anything was going on between them. It doesn't!"

"What do you mean Mandy was acting funny?"

"Excited. Happy. I don't know."

"But you knew it wasn't caused by Richard Ferrell."

She sat down on the sofa and stared at the brown and gold area rug on the floor. She was silent for a long moment, and I thought I was going to have to prod her again. Then she said, "I don't believe it. I don't care what it looks like. I still don't believe it."

Softly, I asked, "What do you think it looks like?"

She lifted her eyes to mine, and I could see that they were full of anger and challenge. "You think Mandy and Jeff have run away together," she said, and her voice was almost an accusation.

"When was the last time you talked to Jeff?"

"Last Wednesday night."

"He hasn't been home since then. He may not have gone home that night."

"I know. I've called and called—"

She broke off and looked down at the floor again.

"I don't like this any more than you do, Lisa," I said, "but I think you should tell me the truth."

Her voice was hushed as she said, "What do you want to know?"

"Barney Wilcox at the Texas Moon told me he saw Mandy and Jeff kissing Wednesday night." I saw her shoulders jerk slightly as I said it. "He said Mandy was very excited and nervous. Was she?"

"They both were."

"Richard Ferrell said Mandy wouldn't go out with him Wednesday night, that she had something else to do, something important. Do you know what it was?"

"No."

"When the three of you came back here, did Mandy tell you that she and Jeff were lovers?"

Her head snapped up. "No!"

"Did they tell you they were leaving together?"

"No! No . . . they didn't have the guts . . ."

I felt like a jackass. Lisa stared up at me, brown eyes wide and starting to fill with tears. In a halting voice, she went on, "They . . . they must've sneaked out later . . . they could've at least told me. Don't you think that would have been the decent thing to do?"

I sighed and sat down in an armchair. "I'm sorry I had to do that, Lisa. I had to get the truth out of you."

"I didn't ask you to sit down!" she snapped. "I didn't ask you to call me Lisa, either. Who do you think you are? My big brother? Or my father, that's more like it."

"Neither of them said anything to you that night about leaving?"

She ignored my question and said, "You want the truth. How can a person tell you the truth when they're afraid to admit it even to themselves? You think I enjoy knowing that my best friend and the man I love have run away together? They're probably in some motel room together right now."

"I guess she wasn't your best friend after all."

"No," Lisa laughed bitterly. "I guess not."

I put my hands on my knees and stood up. "I don't think I'll have to bother you again, Miss Montgomery. I hope not. I'm sorry if I caused you any trouble."

I hadn't caused her troubles. That's just one of the things you say at a time like that. Lisa Montgomery's troubles had started much earlier.

I had the door open and was about to go out onto the front porch when Lisa said, "Will you go on looking for Mandy now?"

"I don't know," I answered honestly. "I'll have to talk to Mrs. Traft and tell her what I think happened. Then it's up to her. If she wants me to keep looking, I'll try to locate Mandy for her. But I'm not going to kidnap anyone who left of their own free will and bring them home."

"That's good. It wouldn't be right to do that."

I nodded and went on out.

The last half hour had been unpleasant, and the immediate future wasn't much more promising. I didn't relish the prospect of telling Gloria Traft that her daughter had probably run off with Jeff Willington and in all likelihood was shacked up with him somewhere. It was a chore that had to be done, though, and you never know how a job's going to turn out when you take it.

I walked back down the street to my car as a chilly breeze whipped fallen leaves around my feet. I hadn't been paying any attention to the weather forecast, but it felt like a cold front had passed through.

When I got back to the car, I glanced around automatically for Ferrell's dark blue Dodge Dart, then remembered that I didn't have to worry about him following me now. I supposed I would have to call him after I talked to Mrs. Traft. I had promised to let him know what I found out, and somehow the idea of being there in person when I told him that his dream girl had run away with another man didn't appeal to me.

I had gone several blocks when I realized that I still didn't know who I had seen talking so excitedly to Lisa that morning. It couldn't have been Jeff Willington, though, so I decided that it was probably unrelated to this mess. And that's what it was, a mess.

Rush hour traffic had started clogging up the streets. When I got to the West Freeway, I could see that the cars on the overpass were already bumper-to-bumper, so I stayed on University and went on under. I could get back to the Traft house in Ridgmar quicker by cutting across on Lancaster and Camp Bowie.

As I went past Trinity Park and the Botanic Gardens, I noticed a silver-blue Corvette behind me in the mirror. When I turned left on Lancaster, it was two cars behind me in the turn lane. I slowed down in front of Will Rogers Coliseum and the other cars went around me, but the Corvette kept its distance. Either they thought I was pretty dense, or they didn't care if I knew they were back there.

I wondered how long they had been tagging me. They could have been following the Dodge Dart and using it as a screen, or they could have just picked me up. I didn't waste much energy trying to figure out who they were, because I didn't have the slightest idea.

Lancaster ran into Camp Bowie and I turned left again. The tail stayed in place, beating the light easily. The tires of my Ford bumped and clattered over the old red brick street as I sped up.

I changed lanes, and the Corvette did, too. If they had been watching Ferrell follow me all day, they might think I was dumb enough not to notice them. I hoped they thought I was dumb.

I slowed down suddenly, letting a yellow light go red and catch me. The trailing car didn't have any choice but to come to a stop right behind me. A quick glance in the rear view mirror showed me two men, but I couldn't distinguish their features very well, especially since the Corvette rode lower to the ground than my car. From what I could see, though, I didn't recognize either one of them.

The decision whether to let it go on or try to lose them had to be made. If I tried to lose them, they would know that I was aware of their presence. If I let it go, I could possibly take them by surprise when I was good and ready, as I had Ferrell. That would be the smart thing to do.

I kept the pace deliberate. Speeding up now would only alert them. If they wanted to follow me, that was fine.

It took me another ten minutes to get to the Traft house. I turned again at the opening in the hedge and parked at the front door. I caught just a glimpse of the silver-blue Corvette going by on the street. It never slowed down. They were either satisfied and were going on, or they were going to park out of sight and wait for me.

The same maid answered my knock and held the door open for me. I stepped inside and said, "I'd like to see Mrs. Traft, please."

"Mrs. Traft is resting right now . . ."

"It's important."

"Just a moment. I'll tell her you're here."

She left me standing in the hall again and went upstairs. I cooled my heels there for almost ten minutes before the maid came back down and said, "If you'll wait in the study, Mrs. Traft will be down in just a few minutes. Could I get you a drink?"

"No thanks."

She opened the study door and I went inside to wait some more. I really didn't mind putting this off. I had no idea how Gloria Traft would react to what I had to tell her.

I ran my eye along the bookshelves as I waited. There was quite an assortment of titles, and I played a little game of trying to guess who read what. There were some textbooks on business management and the oil industry. Those had to belong to Austin Traft. The historical novels could have gone to either Gloria or Mandy, but since Bradbury, Asimov and Heinlein were also in evidence, I gave the nod on the sagas to Gloria. She didn't seem the type to read science fiction. I took down a copy of *The Foundation Trilogy* and opened it to the flyleaf. I was surprised to find Austin Traft's name written in a flowing hand.

The door opened and Gloria Traft said, "Hello, Mr. Cody. Alicia says you have something important to tell me."

I put the book back on the shelf where I had gotten it and turned to face her. There was no point in putting it off. I said, "Mrs. Traft, I think I know what happened to Mandy."

"You've found her?" I hated to see the flash of hope that sprang into her eyes as she said it.

"No, I don't know where she is," I said, "but I think she's all right. I think I know what she did last Wednesday night."

"Well, what is it?" Mrs. Traft's veneer of self-control had cracked since that morning. I could see more lines on her face, more shadows underneath her eyes. She looked like a lady who had spent the day worrying.

"I think Mandy ran away with Jeff Willington," I said bluntly. "I don't know where they are, but I can probably locate them."

The hope in her eyes turned to disappointment. She said softly, "I was hoping you knew where she was. I was hoping you could bring her home to me."

"That's another thing," I said. "I can keep looking, if you want me to, but if I find Mandy and it turns out I'm right, I won't bring her home unless that's what she wants, too. If she's happy where she is, all you'll get from me is that one fact."

I was expecting her to tell me to go to hell, that I was fired. Instead, she laughed, taking me by surprise, a harsh laugh that flirted with the raw edge of hysteria.

"Excuse me," she said. "It's just that I can't believe it. Mandy and Jeff are just friends. She wasn't that interested in him, not seriously."

"Maybe you don't know her as well as you thought. You said that the two of you weren't very close."

"Yes, but I always got the impression that Jeff and Lisa were interested in each other. I even heard some talk about marriage at one time."

"That was at one time. From what I've been told, there was definitely a romance going on between Mandy and Jeff. Lisa all but confirmed it. She doesn't want to admit it to herself, but it's still true."

Mrs. Traft crossed her arms in front of her chest and turned away. She said, "And you think they've left together?"

"Some of Mandy's clothes are gone and there were no signs of trouble. Lisa didn't hear anything. It seems to me that indicates Mandy left of her own free will. No one has seen Jeff since last Wednesday, either. When I found out that they were possibly lovers, it was a reasonable assumption to make that they left together."

She crossed the room to the big desk and picked up a fountain pen, toying with it. "But you don't know where they are now?"

"No. I can probably find them, but it may take a while. They could have gone a long way since last Thursday. I don't see any way I could have Mandy back here by Wednesday, assuming that she wants to come back."

"I suppose it will cost more this way, too."

I looked at her for a minute and then turned to walk out of the study. She said, "Wait, Mr. Cody, please." It was the desperation in her voice that stopped me.

"I didn't mean that the way it sounded," she went on. "I just wanted to know if you needed more money, for expenses and things."

"You want me to stay on the case?"

"Yes, very much." There was an appeal on her face that was urgent. "I want you to find Mandy, more than ever now."

I thought about all the legwork it would involve, all the tedious details. There was no doubt the job would pay well, but would the money be worth it? That's what I had to decide.

I looked at Gloria Traft and said, "Okay, I'll try to find Mandy. But what I said before still goes. I'll bring her back only if she wants to come back. Otherwise, I'll let you know she's all right and what you do then is up to you."

"All right. That's fair enough. You'll get right back to work on it, then?"

"Yes. I won't need any more money yet. I'll let you know when I do."

"What will you do next?"

"Try to trace their movements. I've got the picture of Mandy, and I'll dig up one of Willington. Then I'll cover the neighborhood again, see if I can turn up anybody who saw them leaving. I'll hit the bus stations and the airports. If I can get Willington's license number, I have friends on the police force who can maybe find out if his car has been involved in any wrecks or violations anywhere. It's slow work, Mrs. Traft. Mostly it's just plugging away, trying to take every possibility into account."

She gave me a thin smile. It only made her look more worried and strained. "I have confidence in you, Mr. Cody."

"Thanks," I grunted. I wished I had as much confidence in me as she did.

I left her standing in the study, staring at the rows of books, but I suspected she wasn't seeing them.

The maid, Alicia, showed me out, even though I was learning my way around by now. I stood on the wide front porch for a minute, taking deep breaths of the chilly air. The sun was low in the sky, halfway behind a cloudbank moving in from the west. I could feel a trace of dampness in the air that hadn't been there earlier in the day.

I didn't see the silver-blue Corvette anywhere as I pulled away from the Traft house. Either they had given up the tail, or they were being a lot more subtle about it.

That was one aspect of the case that really puzzled me. I could understand Richard Ferrell following me, but there was no reason for anyone else to be doing it. Not unless there were things swimming underneath the surface of this case that hadn't yet come up for air.

Traffic was still fairly heavy, and it took me over fifteen minutes to get back to my office on Camp Bowie, just up the street from Amon Carter Square and the Museum complex. It was two rooms in the end of a single story building that also housed a camera shop, a second-rate art gallery and a health food store. I had to park in the alley at the side, since the spillover from the other stores always took up the spaces in front of my office.

I unlocked the door that announced my name and profession and went inside. The office was cool. I pushed the thermostat on the heater up and sat down behind the metal desk.

I had been in a hurry that morning to get to my appointment with Mrs. Traft, so I had just dropped the mail on the desk and left it. Now I began to sort through it.

There were some bills and three different brochures trying to sell me office supplies and a ten dollar check from a guy for whom I had done some divorce work. Now he was only six months behind on his payments.

I pulled the telephone over on the desk and called my answering service, to find out that Richard Ferrell had called four times in the last two hours. He must have started calling as soon as he got home.

I got my notebook out and looked up his number. He had to find out about it sooner or later. I decided I might as well get it over with.

He answered before one ring was complete. "Hello?" he said, in a tense, breathless voice.

"This is Cody."

"Mr. Cody! Have you found her? Do you know where she is? Have you—"

"Slow down," I cut in on him. "I don't know where Mandy is, but I think she's all right. You're not going to like what I have to say, though, Ferrell."

"What is it?" His voice was slower now, but still a long way from calm.

I took a deep breath. I was getting tired of breaking this news. "All the evidence indicates that Mandy has run away with Jeff Willington."

"What?"

It was a roar that almost deafened me and left me unprepared for what came next. I could barely hear him as he whispered, "That can't be. I love her. She wouldn't do that."

"Look, Richard," I said, "Willington's been gone since last week, too, and even Lisa thinks there was something going on between them. I don't blame you for not liking it, but it looks like that's what happened."

"She wouldn't do that to me, Mr. Cody. I know she didn't love me, not yet, but she would have in time. She wouldn't just run off that way."

This conversation was getting us nowhere, and there were still things I needed to do before I picked up Janice Bryant for our date. I said, "I'll be in touch with you, Richard. Mrs. Traft still wants me to locate them for her, and when I do, maybe she'd be willing to tell you where Mandy is. That's up to her. I'm sorry it turned out this way."

There was a moment's silence, then Ferrell said, "Mandy and Jeff . . . oh, shit . . ."

He hung up.

That had been a real pleasant conversation. Now I had another one to get out of the way. I needed a picture of Jeff Willington, and I figured Lisa would probably have one. I looked up that number and dialed it.

When there was no answer after fifteen rings I hung up and looked at my watch. It was ten minutes until six. I glanced out the window and saw that the clouds coming in had brought on an early dusk.

I suddenly remembered the Remington prints from the Texas Moon. They were still in the back seat of my car. I went outside and carried the whole armload back in with me, stacking them on the desk.

I wouldn't have room for all of them in my small apartment, but several of them could hang on the walls here. I flipped through them and picked one out, the famous "Stampeded By Lightning" painting. It would look good on the wall behind the desk, over my chair.

I selected three more to go with it and put all four of them in the back room. It was a little after six now. I tried Lisa Montgomery's number again and still got no answer.

There was plenty of time before I had to go home and get ready to pick up Janice. It wouldn't hurt to drive back over to TCU. If Lisa was there by then, I could maybe go ahead and get the picture from her.

Traffic was considerably lighter now. I turned the headlights and heater and radio on, and listened to a sports talk show as I drove toward TCU. The gas gauge showed that the tank was only a quarter full. I started to pull into a station and fill up, then changed my mind. I wanted to get to Lisa's and get it over with.

This would make my third visit of the day. If I hadn't known my way around the neighborhood already, I would have by now. The parking place I found this time was the closest one yet, only two houses away.

There were no lights on in the living room that I could see. As I went up the walk, I could tell that the curtains were half closed.

I knocked on the door and then put my hands back in my pockets. When no one answered the knock, I walked over and leaned down to look in at the window.

There were lights on in the back part of the house, but no movement. Lisa must've left the lights on when she went out. I wondered if I should wait for her to return. She might be back soon, but there was no way of knowing.

I was just about to straighten up when something caught my eye. I leaned closer, almost putting my nose against the screen. In the few seconds before my breath fogged up the window, I saw something that made my heart stop for a second.

Light from the rear of the house spilled out into a hall, and right on the edge of that light were the fingers of a human hand, hooked as if trying to claw into the floor.

The window was fastened with a simple hook and eye. It took only a few seconds for me to slash the screen with my pocketknife, unhook it and lift it away from the window. A kick with my boot shattered the glass.

I bent over to unfasten the latch on the window and almost gagged as gas fumes poured out through the opening I had made. I could tell from the intensity of it that the house was full of the sickly sweet stuff.

There wasn't even time for an unspoken prayer. I raised the window and went in fast, but my head was spinning and my eyes burning before I was halfway across the room. I went on anyway, stooping in the dimness to gather up the soft, limp body on the floor. I found the front door somehow, got it unlocked and staggered with my burden back out into the cold, clean air.

I dropped Lisa on the lawn and fell to the ground beside her. I rolled her over. There was still enough twilight in the sky that I could see how pale she was. I couldn't tell if she was breathing or not. She was wearing a thick bathrobe. I slipped my fingers inside it and found a heartbeat, a weak one, but still there.

I cupped my mouth over hers and started breathing, in and out, in and out. I heard someone say, "Hey, man, what're you doing?" but I didn't look up until Lisa suddenly moaned and started drawing great shuddering breaths on her own.

There were cars slowing down on the street and people standing around now. I recognized some of the neighbors. One boy had a lit cigarette in his mouth. I came to my feet and slapped it out in one motion. He jumped back and cried, "Watch it!"

"You watch it, dammit!" Adrenaline was still racing through me. "That house is full of gas!"

They all gaped at me. I pointed at Lisa and snapped, "For God's sake, somebody call an ambulance!"

An elderly man said, "I'll do it," and started loping back toward his house. I whipped my jacket off, then balled it around my fist. Holding my breath, I ran back to the house and started breaking windows.

Lisa was sitting up, supported by some of the neighbors, when I walked back across the lawn. There was nothing to do now but wait for the ambulance and let the house air out.

Lisa looked up at me. She coughed once, then said, "You should've left me in there."

I could feel nausea, an aftereffect of the gas maybe, creeping up my throat. "Why?" I said harshly. "Just because your boyfriend left you?" Some of the bystanders gave me dirty looks. I didn't think the looks were justified. But they didn't understand.

"It's a reason," she said softly.

I shook my head. "Not a good enough one."

I RODE IN the ambulance with Lisa, but she wouldn't tell me much, just that I should have left her in the house to die. I didn't see much point in arguing with her now. I hoped she would feel differently later. Especially since I felt partially responsible for her state. Forcing her to admit the truth to herself like I had must have been shattering.

I had gone back into the house before the ambulance arrived and lifted the photograph of Friendship that had been in Mandy's desk. I didn't want to ask Lisa if she had any other pictures of Jeff, not now. This one might be better anyway, since it showed Mandy and Jeff together. People might come closer to remembering them that way.

A girl working behind the counter in the emergency room wanted to know who was the next-of-kin or responsible person for Lisa. I remembered her saying that her parents and grandfather were dead, so I gave the girl Mrs. Austin Traft's name. I didn't think Mrs. Traft would mind.

A clock on the sterile white wall told me that it was after seven o'clock. I was supposed to pick up Janice Bryant at seven thirty, and I would never make it. I found a pay phone while a white-coated intern with a beard was checking Lisa over.

Janice answered on the third ring, saying "Hello?" in her cool voice.

"Hi, this is Cody," I said. "I'm sorry, but I've been held up. I'm afraid I'm going to be a little late."

"All right. Is anything wrong?"

"It's just this case I'm working on. A girl tried to commit suicide. I'm at the hospital with her now. I think she's going to be all right."

There was a little silence on the other end of the line, then Janice said, "You do lead an interesting life, Mr. Cody. I'll forgive you for being late if you promise to tell me all about it."

"Sure. I don't mind rehashing all the sordid details."

I don't know what made me say it. A desire to ruffle her placid exterior, maybe. I halfway expected her to hang up on me, and I was already biting my tongue.

"And I don't mind hearing them. Are they nice and gruesome?" she purred. I was no match for her.

"I'll be there by eight or a little after," I said.

"Goodbye, Mr. Cody."

I stared at the phone for a second before I hung up and shook my head.

I turned around to see the intern standing there waiting for me. I could still smell medical school on him, but he had an air of emerging competence. He said, "You were with that girl who was brought in earlier, weren't you?"

"That's right. How bad was it?"

He shrugged. "Pretty bad. She might not have lasted much longer. But she's young, and her respiratory system is in good shape. She'll make it, I think. How did she do it? Stove?"

"Yeah. Blew out the pilots and turned everything on full blast. We were lucky nothing set it off."

"When a house full of gas goes up, it can take a whole block with it sometimes."

"I guess she didn't think of that."

He told me where to go to find the admissions office. I got a room for Lisa for the night, using Gloria Traft's name again. I hoped she wouldn't mind footing the bill.

The last I saw of Lisa that night, she was lying in a hospital bed, sleeping from the sedation she had been given. The curtain between the beds was drawn, and the other woman in the room was watching television.

I stood there for a moment and thought about what kind of love it would have to be to make a person want to take her own life when it was denied. It would have to be a very strong love and a very proud one. Too proud. I reached out and touched the sleeping girl's cheek with my fingertips before I left the room.

I made a flying trip to my apartment, unloading the Remington prints, showering and shaving quickly and dressing in one of my nicer outfits. It consisted of dark slacks, a tan turtleneck and a brown leather jacket. I decided the boots didn't look too bad and put them back on.

It was three minutes after eight when I rang the bell of Janice Bryant's Westover Hills home. She opened the door and looked dazzling in a beige dress that seemed to float around her. She smiled and said, "Hello. Is everything under control now, Mr. Cody?"

"Make it just Cody. Yes, and I'm sorry about the way I sounded on the phone earlier . . ."

"Don't worry about it, Cody. Just ply me with *haute cuisine*." One eye closed in an exaggerated wink. "Who knows what might happen?"

I couldn't stop a grin from breaking out on my face. She made me feel good. I could almost forget about Mandy Traft, and Jeff, and Lisa. Almost.

She closed the door and we went back down the walk to my car. Janice said, "What high-class dreadfully expensive restaurant are you taking me to, Cody?"

"Well, I know this place I think you'll like. It's got these big golden arches out front, see . . ."

Actually, we wound up eating steak and seafood. It was good, and so was the company. Janice didn't make any effort to learn more about Lisa's suicide attempt, and I kept the conversation off the other aspects of the case. Janice knew more about Western art than anyone else I knew, and our conversation was heavily flavored with names like Remington and Russell. It was a very interesting hour.

It wasn't until we were relaxing over after-dinner drinks that anything related to the day's events came up. That was when I said, "Tell me about your new job. Barney Wilcox seems like a pretty nice guy."

"He is. My official title is Personal Assistant. It's a good job, and when Barney offered it to me one night a few weeks ago when I was in the club, I took it."

I sipped my drink and asked, "What exactly do you do?"

"Oh, I handle correspondence, do telephone work, little things that free Barney to supervise the remodeling. The Texas Moon is going to be the best disco in the state. Much better than anything in Dallas or Houston."

"Oh," I said perversely, "you're a glorified secretary."

For a second, I think she was torn between laughing out loud and throwing her drink in my face. Then she showed her even white teeth in a smile, and the laugh won. It was one of the first genuine laughs I had heard from her.

"Cody," she said, "are you always so rude?"

"Only to people I like." I smiled back at her.

After that, we stopped sniping at each other. I was starting to feel more comfortable around her. Given time, I decided, the relationship might develop into something.

"Why are they changing the Texas moon into a disco?" I asked. "The place was bad enough the way it was."

"You didn't like it?"

"It was trying to be something that it really wasn't. The kind of Texas that it represented never really existed."

"What's wrong with fantasy?"

"Nothing. I just hate to see a good place's image exploited."

"Then it's exploitation you dislike, not fantasy."

"Yeah. I guess so."

"And you think it'll be even worse as a disco, right?"

"If they're going to retain the Texas imagery, I do. Mindless music, inane catchphrases, meaningless sexuality . . . Texas was a good place to live before it started trying to be another California or New York. Now it just takes the latest fads and crazes and slaps plastic longhorns on them. Maybe it's a lot slicker place now, but it's also a lot less real."

Janice looked into my eyes and said slowly, "Cody, you sound old."

I nodded glumly. "God, don't I know it."

"So cheer up. The world's not really as bad as all that. Isn't good food and the company of a beautiful woman proof enough of that?"

"I guess so." She had me smiling again. "That looked like a pretty expensive proposition that Wilcox is setting up. Can he afford it?"

"I suppose he can. He's doing it, isn't he? I think he has some silent partners who are putting up some of the funds. I'm not familiar enough with the business yet to be sure. You're right, though. It's going to be very expensive."

We finished our drinks and I paid the tab. It took a pretty healthy bite out of my ready cash, but I had Mrs. Traft's two thousand dollar retainer to deposit the next day. I paused at the pay phone just inside the restaurant door and said, "Do you mind if I check with my answering service? When I've got a case working, I like to keep track of my calls."

"Not at all."

As I dropped coins in the slot and dialed, I thought about how nice the evening had been. Despite the events of the day, being with Janice had given me an overall boost in spirits. She had shown a definite interest in me, and the verbal jousting had only livened things up.

When my service answered, I said, "This is Cody. Any calls?"

"Yes, a Mrs. Traft called three times. She said it was urgent, and she sounded very upset. She wanted you to call her back as soon as possible."

"Okay. Anything else?"

"No, sir."

I said thanks and hung up. Digging for more change, I said to Janice, "My client wants me to call her."

"Something important?"

"I don't know." The phone was ringing at the Traft house now. "It's supposed to be urgent. Who knows what that means?"

A quiet female voice answered the phone. I recognized it as the maid's, who was evidently a live-in. "Austin Traft's residence."

"This is Cody," I said. "Mrs. Traft wanted me to call her."

"Mr. Cody!" The controlled voice showed sudden signs of worry and strain. "I'm so glad you called. I had to call the doctor for Mrs. Traft. He's with her now."

"What is it? What's wrong?"

"This afternoon, Mrs. Traft received a phone call that made her very upset. Earlier this evening, a package arrived for her that seemed to . . . well, push her over the edge. She was very nearly hysterical."

"What was in the package?"

"I don't know. She wouldn't say, and she's kept it with her ever since. She tried to call you, and when she couldn't reach you, she got in such a state, I didn't know what else to do but call her doctor."

"Does she still want to see me?"

"She did earlier, very much so, in fact. She said you had to help her. I think it might reassure her if you were here."

"Okay. What time was that phone call this afternoon, before or after I was there?"

"Before."

That was why Gloria Traft had looked and acted so tense during our last meeting. She had heard something during the phone call that had nearly knocked her for a loop. Whatever was in the package had finished the job.

"All right," I told the maid. Janice had moved closer and was making no secret of the fact that she was listening to my end of the conversation. I looked a question at her as I said into the phone, "I'll get right over there."

"And you'll take me with you," Janice said as soon as I had hung up.

"I could drop you off at your house. It wouldn't be out of the way."

"No, sir. I've never seen a private detective in action before."

"Most of the time, action in this job consists of sitting and waiting."

"Not always, though."

"No," I admitted. "Not always."

I made good time to Ridgmar, filling Janice in on the case as I drove. Monday night traffic was fairly light. I parked in front of the Traft house and opened the car door for Janice. The maid had the front door open and was waiting for us before we were even on the porch.

"How's Mrs. Traft?" I asked as soon as we were inside.

"She's sleeping. The doctor gave her a sedative. He just left."

"Is there anything I can do?"

"She gave him the package and told him to put it in the study. She told him not to open it." The maid frowned. I remembered her name was Alicia. "Mrs. Traft said no one was to open it but you. She said you would take care of it."

"Did she tell the doctor what the phone call this afternoon was about?"

"No."

"I guess I'd better take a look at this package."

Alicia started to show me to the study, then remembered that I knew where it was. I led the way in. Janice came along quietly behind me.

The package was sitting on the desk. It was small, about three inches by six inches and maybe two inches deep. Brown wrapping paper was folded around it, but I could tell that it had already been opened. I picked it up, surprised by its light weight, and saw Mrs. Traft's name written in felt tip pen on the wrapping paper. "How was this delivered?" I asked.

"There was a knock on the door," Alicia said. "I answered it and saw the package lying there, but there was no one else around."

I grunted and started taking the paper off. Inside was a plain white cardboard box. I lifted the top off.

The slip of paper inside was the same size as the box. What looked like the same felt tip pen had printed on it in square black letters:

WE TOLD YOU WE HAVE YOUR DAUGHTER.
HERE'S PROOF. HAVE $125,000 IN CASH READY
TOMORROW. WE'LL TELL YOU WHAT TO DO
WITH IT. SMALL BILLS ONLY. NO POLICE.

I lifted the paper and looked at what was underneath it, nestled on a bed of cotton.

Janice looked over my shoulder and said, "Oh, my God," in a very small voice.

Inside the box was a girl's finger.

CHAPTER III

I PUT THE paper back in the box and put the lid on it, then set it down on the desk. I could feel Janice's fingers digging into my arm. Her voice had lost every bit of its cool sophistication as she said, "Cody, was that . . .?"

"It was."

I turned around and saw that Alicia had followed us into the study. By the look on her face, I knew she had seen what was inside the box, too. I said, "Do you want to call the police, or would you rather I did it?"

"I—I don't know. I thought Mrs. Traft wanted you to handle things. I don't think she wanted the police."

"That was fine when it was just a missing person case," I said. "I was willing to go along with that, but if I have knowledge of a kidnapping, it could cost me my license to cover it up. And I have no intention of losing my license."

There was a phone on the desk. I reached for it.

Janice stopped me. "Wait, Cody. If you call the police, won't it put the girl in danger? The note warned Mrs. Traft about that."

"Ransom notes always do. Mandy is already in danger, and the cops have a lot better chance of getting her out of it than I do."

"Mrs. Traft put it in your hands," the maid said.

"That's right," Janice agreed.

I turned my back toward them and started to dial, but my finger kept going slower. I hung up before I finished the number.

"All right," I said. "I suppose I can think about it for a minute."

I sat down in the big chair behind the desk and tried to concentrate. It looked like my theory about Mandy and Jeff running away together was out the window. This development punched a gaping hole in it. Unless . . .

I had no way of knowing that the finger in the box had belonged to Mandy Traft. A couple of kids running away might come up with some pretty desperate ideas when their money ran out.

There was an ache developing around my temples. If the snatch was for real, that left the problem of Jeff Willington's disappearance. Would he kidnap his own lover? What if they had been in on it together and then Mandy tried to back out? There were just too many different ways it could work.

Maybe I could find something in Jeff's apartment that would show me a trail. There had been nothing here or at the house near TCU to indicate anything other than that Jeff and Mandy had run away together. But the inside of Jeff's apartment was still unknown territory.

An unsettling thought occurred to me. I had been at Jeff's twice. He and Mandy could have been on the other side of the door both times. It wasn't likely; it would be a bad place for them to hide, but nothing was impossible. I wanted to have a look around the place, anyway.

I stood up and said, "Come on, Janice. I'll take you home."

"You're not going to call the police?"

"Not yet. I want to check on some things first. If I don't find anything in a hurry, though, I won't have any choice."

"When Mrs. Traft wakes up, I'll tell her you're handling things," Alicia said.

Janice made a slight face as I picked up the box and slipped it into my jacket pocket. "Safekeeping," I said in answer to Alicia's puzzled look.

When we were back in the car, I noticed that Janice wasn't sitting as close to me as she had before. The price you pay for carrying a human finger in your pocket, I guess.

"What are you going to do?" she asked as I piloted the car back toward her house.

"I want to take a look around Jeff Willington's apartment," I said. "I still feel like he's mixed up in this some way. Until tonight, what little evidence there was suggested that he and Mandy ran off together."

"What if you don't find anything?"

"I'll have to call the cops and turn it over to them. I can't do Mandy Traft any good butting my head against a brick wall."

I pulled up in front of Janice's house and started to get out. She put a hand on my arm and said, "That's all right. I can get in by myself. You need to hurry."

"Okay. Thanks. Sorry the evening ended up like it did."

"Cody . . ."

There was a streetlight not far away and its glow let me see the concern on Janice's face as she looked at me. "Kidnappers are usually dangerous men, aren't they?" she continued.

"Usually."

She leaned toward me, and I felt her lips on mine. They were warm and soft and felt better than I had ever imagined they would. We kissed for a moment that wasn't long enough, then she pulled away and said quietly, "Be careful."

"I will."

My headache had subsided briefly, but it came back as I drove away from Janice Bryant's house.

It didn't take long to get to the apartments where Jeff lived. I parked on the street, put the little box in the glove compartment behind a box of Kleenex and hurried into the courtyard. Most of the apartments had lights on in them. I went past the manager's apartment without pausing and took the metal stairs as quickly as I could without making a lot of racket.

I could feel my pulse speeding up with every step I took as I walked down the balcony. The temperature had dropped enough since sundown that my breath hovered in the air in front of me in feathery plumes.

There were lights on in both apartments that flanked Jeff's, but Number 27 was dark and quiet. TV noises came from Mrs. Lansing's, and on the other side, I could hear Becky Roberts and a man that I hoped was her husband talking in loud voices.

I stood in front of the door to Jeff's apartment for several seconds, straining my ears to hear any sound that might come from within. None did. I put my hand on the knob and tried it gingerly.

The door was locked, as I had figured it would be. Getting inside would constitute Breaking and Entering. If I was caught, that would make a nice companion piece with Concealing Evidence.

A credit card would get me past the lock. If the place was as deserted as it looked, then the chain wouldn't be on.

As I worked with the lock, I began to wish that my .38 wasn't back in my own apartment. It had been nearly a year since I had carried it, though, and the thought of picking it up simply hadn't occurred to me.

I was out of practice, and the plastic card kept slipping in my fingers. It took me almost three minutes to get the door open. The lock finally snicked back, though.

I put a hand on the door and gave it a push, then jerked back to one side. Nothing happened, except that the door opened.

I waited for a long moment, heart pounding, then went in, crouching low and almost running. I stopped just inside the door and tried to penetrate the darkness with my eyes.

The apartment was as quiet and still as it could be. After a minute of standing there and listening, I went back to the door and closed it. I had the small flashlight I usually carried in the car in my pocket. I took it out and snapped it on, shielding the beam partially with the fingers of my other hand.

The light it gave off let me see my way around. I was in the living room. The furniture had that well-worn look it always takes on in furnished apartments, but there was nothing out of the ordinary. A narrow bar to my left separated the room from the tiny kitchen.

I went in there and shone the light around. There were no dirty dishes on the bar or in the sink, nothing to indicate that Jeff had left suddenly or unexpectedly. I opened the refrigerator and put the toe of my boot on the little button at the bottom of the door so that the light wouldn't come on.

There was a package of bologna and a loaf of bread on the rack inside. Both had things growing on them. There was a box of milk in the door. I opened it and sniffed and made a face. It looked like Jeff really had been gone since last Wednesday night.

I let the refrigerator door shut softly and moved back into the living room. In the dim glow of the flashlight, I could see that there was nothing personal in the room, only the furnishings that had come with the apartment. I went down a little hall and found the bathroom and bedroom.

The medicine chest in the bathroom was empty. It was starting to look very much like Jeff Willington had moved out for good. I wondered if his disappearance and Mandy's were unconnected. It seemed doubtful that the long arm of coincidence would stretch that far.

I went over the bedroom next. The bed was neatly made. I opened the closet and peered inside. It was empty except for two wire hangers with nothing on them. There were no clothes or shoes to be seen.

A chest with four drawers in it was all that was left in the room. I opened the drawers from top to bottom, finding nothing. I squatted on my heels, looking into the bottom one, and tried to think of a way to report this whole thing to the cops without getting in trouble myself.

Frustrated, I started to shove the drawer back in with a little more force than was necessary. It hung momentarily, and then there was the sound of paper tearing. I frowned and started to pull the drawer out again, more carefully this time.

I had to take the drawer completely out to find the envelope that had slipped underneath it somehow. One corner had been torn almost all the way off, but the sheet of paper inside wasn't damaged.

Jeff Willington's name and address were on the outside. I recognized the return address as being that of the house where Mandy and Lisa lived. The envelope was pale blue, made of thick, glossy paper, and a slight scent of perfume still clung to it. It was postmarked Saturday, October 14. That was five days before Mandy and Jeff had disappeared.

The hand that had addressed it was feminine. I pulled out the letter inside and unfolded it. Small writing covered the whole page. I glanced down at the signature. It read, *I love you forever — Mandy.*

I went back to the top of the page and started reading.

Dearest, Jeff,

I'm in bed now, and I'm thinking of you. I'm thinking of you in bed with me. I'm thinking about the way I feel when you're with me and we're alone, about the way your body feels and the way you make my body feel.

It occurred to me that maybe I should feel embarrassed. The letter went on in the same passionate vein for several more paragraphs. I scanned through them, looking for anything that might be important. A mention of Lisa caught my eye, and I concentrated on that.

I hope Lisa doesn't take it too hard when we tell her. You would think she'd understand by now. We've done everything but hit her over the head with it. But no, she still thinks the two of you are madly in love!

It's a pity we'll have to break up the trio. Duets are more fun, though. At least we'll get to end it with a job in a nice place.

I don't see why she can't just let you go! I guess we'll just have to be blunt with her. Hope it doesn't hurt her too bad.

Oh, no, it didn't hurt her, I thought. It just made her want to trade her life in for oblivion. I went on reading.

I'll tell her if you don't want to. I really think we should tell her together, though. How mad can she get when she sees she can't fight it? Anyway, I know I don't want us to be apart anymore.

I want us to be together always, and that's the way it's going to be!

Mandy was a girl who got what she wanted, all right. She was used to it, and she wouldn't have it any other way.

This time maybe it hadn't worked out, though. There was no doubt in my mind that she and Willington had planned to run away together, but whether or not they had succeeded was another question.

Suppose the snatch was real and Jeff had stumbled onto it. The kidnappers would have had to dispose of him. They might've known about the plan to run away. They could have cleaned out Jeff's apartment, making it look like he had left on his own, and anyone looking into either disappearance would come to the same conclusions I had earlier. It was an excellent way to stifle pursuit until they were good and ready to present their demands.

Of course, I could be wrong, and the kidnapping could be a phony. Jeff and Mandy might be sitting in a hotel room right now, having a good time and waiting for the hundred and twenty-five grand they were going to rip off from her folks.

But somehow I doubted it. Without ever meeting them, I still didn't think they were the type to pull something like that. A little callous and selfish for the way they had treated Lisa, perhaps, but I didn't think they were devious enough to stage a fake snatch.

I wanted to talk to Mrs. Traft. I wanted to find out exactly what had been said and by whom during that unsettling phone call.

I scanned the rest of the letter without finding anything important, then put it back in the envelope and put the envelope in my pocket. There was nothing else I could do here. I decided to head back for the Traft house. I would wait a little while longer, at least, before I brought the police in on it. I wanted to talk to Gloria Traft first.

Stepping out of the bedroom and into the hall, I clicked the flashlight off. I could find my way out without it, especially since I could see a small strip of light around the door.

As I walked toward it, the strip of light got bigger. I stopped, but it kept getting bigger. The door was opening. I started backing up.

The only problem with that was that one of them was already inside and grabbed me from behind.

I threw myself to one side, tearing at the arms that encircled me. My shins banged against something, and I couldn't stop myself from falling.

My shoulder hit a chair as I fell. I landed hard, and the guy landed on top of me. He let go with one hand and used it to pound me in the ribs. I tried to roll away from him.

The second one was targeted momentarily against the open door. I raised a leg with a still throbbing shin and snapped a kick at his knee as he reached for me. It missed, taking him in the thigh, but it was still enough to knock him back a few steps.

The other guy quit punching me and looped an arm around my neck. It clamped down on my throat just as I exhaled. I was caught with empty lungs.

I got my hands and knees underneath me and went to the side in a heaving dive. The guy went with me. We crashed into what felt like a coffee table, and the arm around my neck suddenly came loose. I rolled away, gasping for air, and lashed out with both fists.

Neither one connected, so I rolled a few feet further and came to my feet rather shakily. The apartment was too dark to see anything but dim shapes, but two of those dim shapes were coming toward me.

I put my hands in my pockets and didn't come up with anything but a butane lighter. I held it out in front of me and said in as menacing a voice as I could manage, "All right, hold it."

They paused just for a second. One of them chuckled and said, "Come on, bud, don't try to scare us." They started forward again.

I waited until they were close, maybe four feet away, then flipped the lighter on. They had figured I was bluffing empty handed, and the sudden flare took them by surprise. They flinched back and apart from each other, just enough to give me an opening.

I took that opening just like a halfback hitting a hole in the line. They grabbed for me and missed, and then I was through the door and pounding down the balcony as hard as I could. Heads were popping out of doors and somebody inquired in a loud, angry voice, "What the hell's going on out there?"

My two attackers probably thought I was trying to get away. I was thinking about the big crescent wrench under the front seat of my car.

I could hear them coming after me. I went down the stairs in a hurry. My car was only about twenty yards away now, and I went into a sprint.

When I got there, I jerked the front door open and dived after the wrench. I never thought to look in the back seat until a cold, hard circle pressed itself against my head.

A voice said, "Be still." I was still.

Footsteps pounded up. My pursuers had arrived. One of them said, "Thanks, boss. We got him now."

The gun went away from my head. Strong fingers clamped down on my shoulders and jerked me out of the car. I caught a glimpse of the man sitting in the back seat before the door was closed and the light went out.

He had a dark, broad face and hair so black it looked like shoe polish. What I could see of his suit looked expensive. The gun he held casually in his thick fingers was a .32. I had never seen him before.

"Let's take him home," he said. "Somebody may have called the cops by now." His voice was quiet, but it had an arrogant power to it.

I tried to twist away from the steely grip that held me. A grating voice said, "Not this time, friend."

The swish of cloth and air warned me, but I couldn't duck in time. Something exploded behind my left ear, and my knees started to buckle. I tried to peer through the shower of sparks that suddenly appeared in front of my eyes, but all I could make out was a silver-blue Corvette parked next to my Ford.

It faded to black, just like everything else.

I HAD BEEN knocked unconscious before, and the first sign of returning to the world had always been the pounding of the blood in my head. That's why I wasn't surprised to hear it this time.

The funny thing was, it kept up, even when feeling was flowing back to my arms and legs. Another noise joined it and formed a harsh, raucous counterpoint to the driving beat. I finally realized that it was music, and it wasn't in my head.

My nose was pressed against something hard and cold and grimy. I opened my eyes and saw that it was a tile floor. I wiggled my fingers and toes to be sure that everything worked, then started to get up on my hands and knees slowly.

A weight landed on my neck, driving me back down. My chin bounced off the floor, and I tasted blood in my mouth. The thing on the back of my neck was a shoe.

"You just stay still. We ain't through with you."

I lay there with the foot on my neck for what seemed like an hour. Nausea was boiling around in my stomach, and it felt like a vise was wrapped around my temples.

My vantage point was about as bad as it could be, but I could see a little bit of the room. It seemed to be long and narrow. The walls were tile, too, and I thought I could see the bottom of a toilet out of the corner of my eye. There were no feet on the floor in front of me, and I heard only a few noises behind me. It seemed likely that the guy standing on me was the only other occupant of the room. I was too weak and sick to do anything about it, though.

Finally, a door opened, and the rock music got louder for a second until it closed. It sounded like a live band doing a poor rendition of "Johnny B. Goode."

"Has he been behaving?" the newcomer asked. I recognized the voice of the man who had been waiting in the back seat of my car.

"He ain't had any choice."

"You can let him up now."

The weight went away from my neck. I moved my head slowly from side to side, wincing at the pain that shot through it. I wondered if I had a concussion. It suddenly seemed like staying on the floor would be the easiest thing to do.

Except that they weren't going to let me stay there. The newcomer's shoes, expensive black ones, came over and prodded me in the ribs. "On your feet, friend."

I put my hands on the floor and shoved. It took forever, but I made it to hands and knees, and then to my feet. The room spun a little bit, but when it settled down, I saw that I had been right. A stall with a toilet in it was at the far end of the room. I had been lying in front of a row of urinals.

"I thought this would be an appropriate place for a business meeting with you."

I swung my eyes over and focused on the man in the blue suit. He was smiling, and on his thick face, the smile was a leer.

His lieutenant was smiling, too, and it didn't look any better on him. He was tall and wide, wearing a cheap suit and looking like he had come straight from Jersey. His one concession to local color was a string tie that made him look about as Texas as those plastic longhorns.

Myself, I didn't feel like smiling. I spat blood on the floor instead.

"Who the hell are you?" the boss said.

"I could ask you the same thing." It surprised me how hoarse my voice was.

"I'm the man who's going to ask the questions, and you're the man who's going to answer them. I know damn well you must be a private cop. What's your name?"

"Sam Spade."

"Hit him, Shelley."

Shelley hit me. He was fast for a man that big. His punch sank into my stomach, doubling me over and puffing all the wind out of me. Shelley wouldn't let me fall down, though. He grabbed my collar and jerked me back up straight.

I tried to catch my breath, and when I had drawn in a couple of lungfuls, I said, "Shelley, huh? As in Percy Bysshe?"

Shelley looked at the boss, and the boss nodded. Shelley hit me again. I wished he would just let me fall down, so I could pass out and get it over with.

"There's no point in being stubborn," the boss said. "This would be a lot simpler if you would tell me your name."

I didn't think my belly could take another one of Shelley's pile drivers. I said, "Cody."

"All right, Cody, that's better. You're a private detective, aren't you?"

I nodded.

"We've been watching you. Are you working for Mrs. Traft?"

"That's none of . . . your business."

The band had finished "Johnny B. Goode" and gone into something I didn't recognize. They weren't any better at it, whatever it was.

"Listen," the boss said, "there's no reason this can't be working out. We don't want to cause you any trouble, Cody. We just don't want you causing us any."

They had been watching me, all right. I cursed myself for not looking beyond Richard Ferrell and spotting the other tail. There was a good chance I was looking at Mandy Traft's kidnappers. No wonder they didn't want me poking around.

I didn't say anything; I just stared at the boss while Shelley kept his heavy hand on my collar. After a moment, the boss said, "Maybe I was wrong about you, Cody. You don't like being slapped around. It just makes you mad. You're not afraid of us, are you?"

I was as scared as I'd ever been, but I tried to keep it from showing. If he thought I might cooperate, he might be a little less careful about what he said.

"Damn right it makes me mad," I growled. "But I don't want to make trouble for anybody, least of all me. Why don't you just tell me what you want?"

"Are you working for Mrs. Traft?"

"Yeah. I guess I can tell you that much."

"What did she hire you to do?"

"That sort of thing is usually confidential. Clients have a right to privacy."

His leer got bigger. "Only if the guy asking the questions is a cop or a lawyer. I'm neither."

I didn't need him to tell me that. I ran my tongue over dry lips. "She hired me to find her daughter. The girl's disappeared."

"See how easy that was? Let him go, Shelley."

Shelley let me go and I rolled my shoulders to ease the stiffness in them. The boss went on, "Yeah, I think I was wrong about you, Cody. Maybe you'd rather talk this over in my office."

"Is the decor any better?"

He chuckled, but his eyes stayed just as dark and hard. He went to the door, pushed it open a few inches and said, "Frank."

Another one the size of Shelley came in. I figured they were the two I had wrestled with in Jeff Willington's apartment. If they were the ones who had snatched Mandy, and Jeff walked in on it, the kid wouldn't have had a chance.

Frank and Shelley flanked me as the boss led us out of the washroom and into a hall. The loud music was coming from behind a door at the far end, but the boss turned the other way, toward another door.

The four of us went through it into an office. There were several filing cabinets, a functional metal desk with an executive chair behind it, and several straight-backed wooden chairs. The boss went behind the desk, and Frank and Shelley sat me down in front of it. They backed away to stand guard in the corners behind me.

The boss put his palms down on the desk and said, "This is better, isn't it? No reason we can't be civilized about this. Have you found the girl yet?"

I had been thinking furiously. They might not know that I was aware of the kidnapping. I stood a lot better chance of coming out alive if they thought I knew nothing about it.

I said, "No, but I know what happened to her."

"Oh? What's that?"

"She ran off with the Willington kid. That was his apartment you grabbed me in. I don't know where they went."

"Does Mrs. Traft want you to find them?"

"She did. I told her I didn't want to. The girl's old enough to make up her own mind about where she goes and who she goes with."

"What did Mrs. Traft say to that?"

"She offered me more money."

"How much more?"

"Two grand." I thought that sounded reasonable.

"And you turned it down?"

"Yeah."

He opened a drawer in the desk, took out a sheaf of one hundred dollar bills and started counting. He stopped when he reached fifty. "That should be plenty," he said, "even though I'm not sure I believe you turned the other down."

"What's it for?"

"I'm hiring you to not look for Mrs. Traft's daughter."

"Why?"

"Do you always ask the client why he wants something done?"

"Usually."

"No wonder you don't look rich." He pushed the stack of bills toward me. "You going to take it or not?"

I reached out slowly, so as not to alarm Shelley and Frank, and picked up the money. "I'll take it," I said. "You just hired yourself a bloodhound with a stopped-up nose. Can I get out of here now?"

"I think so."

I stood up. The two bruisers moved in closer to me.

The boss went on, "It's just that you have one little failing, Cody."

"What's that?"

"You look like an honest man. That makes somebody like me have to be very careful when dealing with you. I have to be convinced that you're capable of corruption."

"I'm playing straight with you. I took your money, didn't I? I won't look for the girl."

"Honest in your dishonesty, eh?" He raised a finger, and Shelley and Frank came closer. "I want you to be sure to remember who your employer is now. Boys, impress it on him."

Some of my strength had returned, enough so that I didn't like the idea of being roughed up again. I half turned where I could see all three of them and said, "That's not necessary."

The boss just said, "Do it."

They both grabbed for me. I ducked and avoided Shelley's lunge, but Frank got a hand on my shoulder and spun me around. He threw a looping punch that landed on my already sore stomach.

Shelley got hold of my other shoulder and turned me again. His punch clipped my jaw, and the floor came up to meet me in a hurry.

I sure as hell wasn't strong enough to fight both of them. I sagged on the floor, hoping they would back off. They didn't. They both had to kick me first. Splinters of pain shot out from my ribs.

"All right," the boss said, "that's enough here. Take him somewhere else and work him over good. I don't want him hanging around the Trafts anymore."

They got on either side of me and picked me up by the arms, being none too gentle about it. The shoulders didn't feel dislocated, but they were wrenched and throbbing. It was all I could do to stay on my feet.

They marched me to the door of the office. The boss opened it, and I was shoved out into the hall. Shelley came out first after me, with Frank right behind him, and I took the only chance I had. While Shelley was still blocking the door, I kicked him in the groin as hard as I could.

It wasn't much of a kick, but they didn't seem to be expecting any resistance, and it landed on target. Shelley yelped and stopped in his tracks. I turned and went down the hall in a staggering run, aiming for the door with the music behind it.

I heard them starting after me, then flung the door open and the music drowned out all other sounds. My eyes had to adjust, and that slowed me down. The hall had been dimly lit, but the room beyond was darker still.

Except for a ring of light that illuminated a stage on the other side of the room. The band was on the floor beside the stage. In the center of the light was a young girl with long red hair, writhing to the music. A tiny G-string was all she wore. The floor between was filled with tables and eagerly watching men.

I didn't have time to take in the show. I started plowing through the tables, heading for a door that I hoped led outside. The angry shouts of jostled patrons followed me. The band stopped in mid-riff.

I was about halfway across the room and starting to think I might make it when a big man in blue jeans and windbreaker stood up and called, "Hold it there, fella! What's your damn hurry?"

I tried to go around him, but he stuck out an arm like a tree trunk and said, "I asked you a question, sumbitch. You're messin' up a damn good show, you know that? Least you could do is answer me."

The boss shouted from across the room, "Stop him! Hold him!"

A slow smile stretched across the man's face. "Looks like somebody wants to talk to you."

He wasn't going to move, and Frank and Shelley were making their way toward me rapidly. There was nothing else I could do. So I hauled off and punched him in the belly as hard as I could.

He just frowned slightly, and then here came the biggest fist I had ever seen. I tried to get out of its way, but it was moving too fast.

I moved my head enough that he caught me on the cheek, saving myself a broken nose. I landed on my back on the floor. A strobe light was flashing on the ceiling directly above me. Its pulsations were suddenly blotted out by Frank's ugly face. The smile on it only made it uglier.

The stripper screamed as they started kicking me. It was the last sound I heard for a while.

The girl's screams had faded into a dull hum as I passed out. When I came to, I didn't realize it for a moment because another dull hum had taken its place.

Then a series of bumps made me aware that I was in a moving car. My eyes seemed to be glued shut. I moved my hands around feebly and decided that I was lying on the floorboard in the back seat.

I shouldn't have revealed that I was conscious. Blunt fingers tangled themselves in my hair and jerked my head up. Pinwheels of fire sparkled in my brain. Shelley's voice grated, "Finally woke up, huh? You sure as hell ain't no sleeping beauty."

I tried to croak a response and then gave it up as a bad job. The car was still bouncing, and I realized that every muscle in my body was screaming in pain. They had given me a beating to end all beatings. I was surprised that it hadn't ended my life as well.

"This should be okay." Frank's voice told me he must be driving. The car came to a rough stop.

The two of them got out, and then I felt hands on my legs, pulling me from the car. They dumped me in the road roughly, sending new jolts of agony through me.

I was lying on a gravel road, too weak to raise my head away from the sharp little stones cutting into my face. One of the bruisers prodded my side with a foot. I decided that every rib must be broken.

"You think he's learned his lesson?"

"If he hasn't, he's pretty damn dumb."

They each gave me a little kick in parting. Shelley said, "So long, cowboy."

They got back in the car and started it up. Acrid exhaust fumes spewed in my face. The sound of the engine started receding. After a few minutes, I couldn't hear it at all.

Once the sound of the car was gone, I could hear other noises. There was the rustle of brush, the occasional croak of a frog and, ever so faintly, the lapping of water.

There was no way of knowing how long I lay there in the road. I hoped no other cars would come along, because if they didn't see me in time, there would be no way I could get out of their path. It was all I could do for a while to keep on drawing one breath after another.

After what seemed like hours, I finally felt a little strength flowing back into my body. I stored it up, lying as still as I could, until I thought it was time to try to move.

I got my elbows on the road and raised myself just a little bit. My eyes still wouldn't open. I lifted shaking fingers to them and felt the dry, crusty blood that had them gummed together. A long painful gash on my forehead told me the source of the blood.

The effort exhausted me, so I stayed in that position for a while before trying to move again. My ribs didn't hurt quite as bad now. Maybe only half of them were broken.

It took me an hour to develop any kind of locomotion, and that was only a slow crawl. I spent the time while I waited peeling the dried blood off of my eyelids. When I had enough of it off, I forced my eyes open and then had to blink rapidly several times as they started to water.

I couldn't see much more with my eyes open. Trees and brush lined the road on both sides and overhung it, cutting out what little light there was from the moon and stars. The sound of the water seemed to be off to my left. I headed in that direction, pausing every few feet to rest.

When I got off the road, I found a sandy slope dotted with bushes. I started to crawl down it, but then one of my arms went out from under me and I was rolling.

I came to a stop with a splash. My head and shoulders were in water, the rest of me in mud. The water was cold, and the shock of it made me jerk my head up and sent sluggish blood a little faster through my veins.

I pulled myself out of the water. I splashed more of it in my face. It was waking me up. I started to think about getting to my feet.

That took a while, but I managed it eventually. I slogged back up the slope to the road and wondered where to go next.

I had no idea where I was. I could see quite a bit of water, so I was on the shore of a lake, but which one I didn't know, since there were quite a few in the area. I had been hearing tiny rumbling noises for a while, and I finally identified them as the sound of trucks passing in the night. That meant there was a highway somewhere nearby. I leaned against a tree trunk gratefully and waited for the sound to come again.

When it did, I headed in that direction in a slow, shambling walk. I had to stop and lean against a tree every so often to rest, but my progress was better than I had expected.

The road twisted and wound around, following the shoreline of the lake. When I came to a fork, I took the route that went to the right, away from the water and toward the sound of traffic.

The road changed from gravel to asphalt, which made the going easier. I passed an occasional house and thought about stopping, but I rejected the idea when I realized how I must look. What I needed to do was get to a phone.

I passed a fenced in compound with a sign out front. I could barely make out what it said in the dim moonlight—FORT WORTH REHA-BILITATION FARM. I knew then that the lake had to be Lake Worth and that I was headed for the Jacksboro Highway, northwest of Fort Worth.

I made it to the highway half an hour later. Traffic was light, but no one would have stopped to give me a ride, not as bloody and battered as I was.

I stood on the edge of the service road and looked around. There was a Dairy Queen across the highway, closed down for the night, but if I remembered right, there was also a public telephone at the edge of the parking lot. Since I was in no shape to dodge traffic, I waited until there were no cars coming from either direction, then started across the highway.

I made it without any trouble, and there was the phone, just as I had thought. I leaned against its little plastic enclosure and jammed my hand in my pocket, searching for change. My fingers encountered something else and pulled it out.

A wad of hundred dollar bills. I knew without counting that there were fifty of them. A brittle laugh forced itself through my bruised lips.

That five thousand wouldn't do me a bit of good right now. What I needed was a quarter.

I finally found one, deep in my pocket, and dropped it in the coin slot. As I punched out a number, I reflected that the five thousand wouldn't help the man who had given Frank and Shelley their orders, either. He thought he had me paid off and scared off, but he was wrong.

The score had been mounting fast. Mandy Traft, maybe. Jeff Willington, maybe. Myself, for sure. He owed me a lot more than five thousand would take care of.

Janice Bryant answered on the fifth ring. Her voice sounded sleepy but anxious as she said, "Hello?"

"This is Cody," I rasped, sounding like a stranger even to myself. "I need help, Janice."

I must've sounded just as bad to her, judging from the sharp intake of breath. "What is it?"

"I need you to . . . come get me. Some guys . . . beat me up. I don't have my car."

"Where are you?"

"Dairy Queen . . . on Jacksboro Highway. Intersection . . . Farm Road 1886."

"Just out of Lake Worth?"

"Yeah."

Her voice was brisk now. "Should I bring a doctor?"

"No, just come get me."

"You stay right there."

"Don't worry . . . about that. I'll be here."

I hung up. I put my forehead against the cold plastic and closed my aching eyes gratefully. It would take her at least twenty-five minutes to get here. I couldn't stay where I was. A cop could cruise by at any time, and I was in no mood to answer questions. After a moment's rest, I hobbled across the parking lot. There was a big, thick-trunked oak tree just out of the light. I put my back against it. It wasn't long before I had slipped down into a sitting position.

I had to talk to Gloria Traft as soon as possible, to find out if there had been any further contact with the kidnappers. And I had to try to identify the men who had roughed me up. If I knew who they were, I would at least have a lead on the trail to Mandy.

I tried to keep my thoughts going along those lines, but visions of hot water and cool hands and a soft bed kept creeping into my head. In my condition, I was no good to Mandy Traft or anyone else, myself included. I needed someone to bind up my wounds and comfort me. Someone like Janice.

I grimaced and told my mind to quit taking such turns, but it was no use.

Almost before I knew it, with my head resting against the knobby bark of the tree in the shadows, I was asleep.

CHAPTER IV

I WAS DREAMING of soft fingertips and woke to find them stroking my face. I opened my eyes. There was a streetlight behind her, and from this angle it threw a halo of light around Janice's head.

"Hi," I said, thick-tongued.

"Cody," she said, and her voice was shaky, "what happened to you?"

I tried to shrug, but my muscles had stiffened up too much. "A guy wanted to make an impression on me. He had two other guys do it for him."

"We've got to get you out of here." She put a hand on my arm. "Can you stand up?"

"I can try."

"I'm sorry it took so long. When I got here, there was a police car going by, so I had to go on past and then come back. And then I almost didn't see you over here. Be careful."

"It's . . . okay."

With her help, I managed to get to my feet. The world spun crazily for a second, but I held onto her for support and it passed. Still leaning on her, I limped toward the car.

She opened the door on the passenger side. I had a little trouble getting into the low-slung Porsche. My head bumped the roof and it made me see pretty lights again for a second.

When we had me inside, I put my head against the back of the bucket seat and closed my eyes again. The blue glare of the mercury vapor streetlight was hurting them.

Janice closed the door and came around to get behind the wheel. She turned the key and the engine came to life with a roar. "I think I should take you to a hospital," she said.

"No . . . Too much to do. Just need to clean up, get some sleep. I'll be all right."

"Are you sure?"

"Yeah . . . I'm sure."

"You're the hotshot private eye. I guess you know what you're talking about."

She wheeled the car out onto the Jacksboro Highway and headed back toward town. I could feel sleep trying to take over my brain again, so before it could, I told her the address of my apartment house.

"I could take you back to my place," she suggested.

"Some . . . other time," I said. "When I can do the offer justice."

I had my eyes cracked open just enough to see the quick, surprised look she gave me, then the smile that slowly spread on her face.

The ride was, for the most part, hazy to me. While we were moving, it seemed like we would never get there, and when we arrived, it seemed like only seconds had passed since we left the Dairy Queen. Janice parked the Porsche in my usual space, right in front of the door, and that reminded me of my own car. I wondered if it was still parked at the apartment where Jeff Willington lived. That was one of the first things I would have to check on when I felt a little more human. I hoped the cops didn't tow it in. I'd have some sticky questions to answer if they found the ransom note and the finger.

Janice came around, opened the door and helped me get out. It was then that the cramps hit my stomach. I pulled away from her and made it to a flowerbed before I lost the dinner we had had hours earlier.

When it was finally over, I straightened up to find her hovering beside me. I whispered, "Key's in my pocket." I pointed a shaky finger at the right one.

She found it and got the door open. I noticed as I shuffled inside that all the other apartments were dark and wondered for the first time what time it was. Janice flipped on the lights in the living room as we went in, and the clock on the wall told me it was four thirty.

"We've got to get you cleaned up," Janice said. "You really need medical attention, Cody."

"I'll be fine. Bathroom's over there."

She reached inside to turn on the light, then let me go first. I went to the sink and put my hands on it for support. My face stared back at me from the mirror.

I was a mess.

My chin was scraped raw, my nose was puffy, and the cut on my head had bled like mad. No wonder Janice had looked shocked at my appearance.

The first thing to do was get some of the blood off so I could see how bad the damage was. I turned the hot water on and reached for a washcloth. As I did, my sense of balance deserted me and I found myself reeling. Janice grabbed my arm before I fell.

"Look," she said, "I know you're stubborn and masculine, but if you fall on that head one more time tonight, you might not wake up. Now sit down!"

She sat me down on the toilet. I watched as she got a washcloth hot and soapy. It felt like heaven as she used it to sponge my face. I surrendered myself to her ministrations.

"Janice," I said, "you're beautiful."

"Thanks. Be still, please."

"No, I mean it. You really are beautiful."

"That cut looks bad."

"Really, really beautiful."

"Be still, Cody. Damn! Did that hurt?"

I shook my head. It hurt like blazes, but she didn't have to know that.

"I don't think you'll need stitches," she said. "Still, as soon as you get a chance, you'd better let a doctor take a look at it."

"Janice, you are really beautiful," I repeated.

"And you're punchy," she said. She rummaged in my medicine chest for a minute, then said, "Here. Take these." She dropped four white tablets in my hand.

"What are they?"

"Aspirin. You need something stronger, but that's all you've got."

She filled my toothbrush glass with water and handed it to me. I swallowed the aspirin, two at a time, wincing as I put the glass against my puffy lips.

"All right," Janice said. "Now let's get your clothes off."

"Huh?"

"How else can I tell how badly you're hurt?"

"Oh. Yeah."

It was quite a job, and a painful one at that, but we got my jacket and shirt and pants off. I called a halt there.

I was a colorful sight to behold. My torso was covered with bruises of many hues. Added to that was the blood that had leaked from an assortment of cuts and scrapes. Janice shook her head and declared, "You really belong in an emergency room."

"My side hurts."

"I'm not surprised." She knelt beside me and poked around my ribs as gently as she could. It was still enough to make me gasp and close my eyes dizzily.

"You've got cracked ribs in there."

"It's a possibility."

"What do you want me to do about it?"

"Run me a tub of hot water. As hot as possible."

She sighed and shook her head, but she started filling the bathtub. Steam rose from it.

I guess the way I was acting was pretty exasperating. But I knew that if I went to a hospital, there was a good chance I wouldn't come out again for several days. I couldn't afford that. Not with Mandy and Jeff still missing, and not with Shelley, Frank and their boss running around loose.

When the bathtub was full, I said, "Okay. Out."

She turned off the faucets and then swung around to face me with a storm brewing in her eyes. "Dammit, Cody," she said. "I'm not going to have you falling in there and drowning."

"I won't fall in." I stood up in my underwear and socks to show how steady on my feet I was and promptly started swaying.

There wasn't any arguing with her after that. Besides, the water looked too inviting to delay.

When I stepped in with Janice steadying me, I almost yelped from the heat. As I sank down into the water, sore muscles spasmed and jerked. But once I was down and the heat started to soak in, I could feel them begin to loosen and relax. I put my head back and said, "Ohhhh . . ."

Janice sat on the edge of the tub and looked down at me. The look on her face was worried, but the slight smile and the concern in her eyes warmed me almost as much as the water. Her hand was resting on the side of the tub close to my head. I reached up and laid my wet hand on top of it. I didn't think she would mind.

"Thank you," I said.

She started to say something, changed her mind, then said, "Cody, you're . . ." She let it trail off.

"I meant what I said before, about you being beautiful."

"Why don't you close your eyes and try to rest?"

"I'd rather look at you."

She didn't blush or act coy. She sat there, with my hand on hers, while the hot water soaked away some of my aches and pains. There was a mood, a feeling in the air that was delicious and just right and totally satisfying in itself. It almost made the rest of the night worth it, just to have her there with me like that.

It didn't last long enough, but neither of us broke it. We waited for it to dissipate on its own. When it had, she said, "Tell me what happened."

"I went to Willington's apartment and got inside. It had been cleaned out. Whoever did it missed a letter from Mandy to Jeff, though. It told me I was partially right. The two of them did plan to run off together. I don't think they got the chance to, though."

"Mandy was kidnapped first?"

"Yeah. And I wouldn't be surprised if Jeff walked in on it accidentally. They probably had a meeting set up somewhere, and that's where the snatch took place."

"What would the kidnappers want with Jeff?"

"They wouldn't."

She understood what I meant. I could see a tightening of the muscles around her mouth. "What happened then? Who did this to you?"

"Two guys came in just as I was ready to leave and jumped me. They knocked me out and I woke up in some strip joint somewhere. There was a fella there who asked me questions, gave me five thousand dollars and told me to forget about Mandy Traft. Then he had the two goons rough me up some more so I'd be sure to get the message. They dumped me on a back road at the edge of Lake Worth."

Janice shuddered. "Lovely business you're in."

"You get used to it."

"Do you, really?"

"No. Never."

After a moment, she said, "Do you think they were the kidnappers?"

"I don't know who else would feel threatened by my poking around. That's why I've got to get a line on them."

"Are you going to call the police?"

"Not until I've talked to Mrs. Traft. She's still my client. She may want to pay the ransom and try to get Mandy back that way."

"But you don't think it's a good idea, do you?"

"I just don't trust kidnappers."

"Well, it's five thirty in the morning. You can't call Mrs. Traft now. Why don't you try to get some sleep?"

I felt a lot better after soaking, and my mind was clearer, but the aspirin and my exhaustion were taking their toll. I was getting pretty drowsy, so I said, "All right. I don't guess you'd leave the room this time, either, would you?"

"You guess right." She got up and found a thick towel and held it out to me.

I got dried mostly on my own. I wrapped the towel around me and said, "Thanks. I can manage now."

"You're sure?"

"I'm sure."

"All right, if you say so."

She walked out of the bathroom ahead of me. I took one step into the hall and my leg muscles turned to mush again. She grabbed me before I could go down.

"That does it. Come on." She put an arm around my shoulders to support me. "We're going to bed."

"Janice . . ." I said.

"What?"

"You picked one hell of a time to try to seduce me."

I was so groggy I didn't know much after that. I wound up in bed somehow, and then I felt her fingers stroking my face again. Just before I went to sleep, I heard her whisper, "Yes, one hell of a time . . ."

I WOKE UP to sunshine coming in the window and the smell of bacon cooking. I understood then what people meant when they talked about waking up and thinking they were in heaven.

My head was sunk down deep and comfortably in the pillow. I hated to move it, but after that first blissful moment when all had seemed right with the world, I started remembering how things really were. I remembered Mandy and Jeff and Lisa. Twinges of pain started shooting from the cuts and bruises that covered most of my body, and I remembered the man who had ordered the beating. I heard someone moving around the kitchen. I remembered Janice.

I sat up slowly, testing myself as I straightened. My vision blurred a little bit, but it cleared up within seconds. I put fingers to my forehead and found a gauze pad that Janice had taped over the gash. There was a raw ache to the area, but it wasn't as bad as I had expected. It was something I could stand.

There were clean clothes laid out on a chair at the foot of the bed. I pushed the covers back and swung my feet out on the floor. I expected a recurrence of the blurred vision and dizziness when I stood up, but my head stayed clear. I put a hand on the back of the chair for support and looked down at myself.

I had never seen so many bruises on a human body. As I moved around carefully, though, I could tell nothing was broken. I was just very stiff and very sore.

It must have been Janice who put the clothes out for me. She had done a good job of picking them. I climbed into the soft blue jeans and the light blue chambray shirt. There were socks there, too, so I pulled them on and looked around for my boots. They were nowhere to be seen.

I walked into the kitchen in my sock feet and saw several strips of bacon draining on a paper towel. There was already a fried egg on a plate on the little Formica topped table, and next to it was a glass of orange juice. I was surprised to find that I was suddenly starving. Janice wasn't anywhere to be seen.

I wanted to eat, but I also wanted to see Janice. I went through the kitchen and into the living room. She was standing in front of the bookshelves that took up nearly an entire wall.

When she saw me, she put the book she was looking at back on the shelf and said, "Good morning. I fixed you some breakfast."

"I saw." My voice sounded less like the croak of a frog this morning. "Thank you."

"How are you feeling?"

"Better than I expected to. I had a good nurse."

"I'll finish fixing that bacon."

She started to go past me. I put out a hand and stopped her. I had called her out in the middle of the night and she had been taking care of me ever since, and she still looked lovely. I said, "Janice . . . thank you."

She didn't blush or look embarrassed. She just smiled back into my eyes and said, "I'm glad I could help."

I let her go and she went on into the kitchen. I spotted my boots on the floor by the sofa, sat down long enough to pull them on, and then joined her.

"You sit down and eat now," she said. "Do you want me to make you a doctor's appointment?"

"Not now." I sat down and took a long sip of the orange juice. "That's good. Today will be too busy for me to see a doctor. Maybe tomorrow."

"You need to be careful of that head."

"I will be."

I dug into the bacon and eggs. They were delicious, and I was forgetting about some of the aches and pains. Janice sat down across the table from me. Between mouthfuls, I asked her, "Did you have any breakfast?"

She shook her head. "I don't eat breakfast. Bad for the figure."

"There's nothing wrong with your figure. It's a damn good figure."

"Thank you. Flattery always helps. Would you like some coffee?"

"Please."

She poured me a cup, then got herself one. As she sipped on it, she said, "I was looking at your library. You've got quite an assortment of titles."

"I like a lot of different things."

"That's the first time I've ever seen Zane Grey and Hermann Hesse on the same shelf. Have you read all of them?"

"Most of them."

"Cody, I have a feeling that you might be an endless well of surprises."

I grunted, not knowing how to answer that, and finished off the rest of the food.

I realized when I was through that I didn't know what time it was. I could tell by the way the sunlight was coming in the windows that it was still fairly early in the morning. I twisted around and looked at the clock on the stove.

It was nearly nine thirty. I stood up and said, "I've got to make some phone calls."

Janice followed me into the living room. I sat down on the sofa. The phone was on an end table beside me.

"Have you heard anything from the Trafts?" I asked.

"No. The phone hasn't rung. I thought about calling there, but I didn't know what to ask. Are you going over there?"

"I'll have to talk to Mrs. Traft soon. There are some things I want to do first, though."

I called the police department and asked for Lieutenant Franklin in Records. When he answered, I said, "Tom, this is Cody. I need your help again."

"What else is new?"

"Put this through your computer-like mind. Male Caucasian, about fifty, black hair possibly dyed, about five-ten and maybe 230 pounds. He has some connection with a strip joint here in town, I think. There are two goons working for him named Shelley and Frank. You make him?"

"Give me a second. He sounds familiar. You know, Cody, I don't have a file on everybody in this town."

"You should know this one. I think he's the type that might have come to your attention."

"Okay, okay." There was silence on the other end for a long minute, then Franklin said, "Maybe I've got him. Sharp dresser, right?"

"Yeah."

"Arrogant little sucker? Not from around here?"

"That's him."

"Sounds like a guy named Waldo Hollis. Used to be mixed up in the mobs back east. He was an underboss in charge of prostitution. The way I remember the story, he and another guy were in line to fill a vacancy higher up in the organization. The other guy got the job and Hollis moved out to save his own skin. He's got nearly a dozen bars here and in Dallas and in Houston. Vice has busted him several times, but nothing ever stuck."

The man I had seen had been a mob type, all right. I thought about Mandy Traft being in the hands of a man like that, and the back of my neck got cold.

"Thanks, Tom," I said. "That sure sounds like him. Do you know where his clubs are here in town?"

"How about telling me what it's all about first?"

I took a deep breath and held it for a second before I answered him. "I can't. I haven't talked to my client since last night. But I want to find this guy for myself, too. Those boys of his that I mentioned took me to a dance last night, and I didn't like the music."

"Hollis called the tune, huh? Listen, Cody, these are not guys to mess around with. There are several unsolved murders back east that can probably be laid at their feet. Why not give me the details and let us handle it?"

"Just tell me where I can find him, Tom. Either that, or hang up and forget I called."

He grumbled a minute, then said, "All right. I warned you. Hollis owns two clubs here. The Banjo Room on East Lancaster and the Emporium on Main Street downtown."

"Are either of them a strip joint?"

"Both of them."

"Okay, thanks."

"Cody—"

"Yeah?"

"I'd hate to have to file a report listing you as the victim. This isn't the wild days anymore. Take it easy, okay?"

"Sure, Tom. Just like always."

I hung up before he could start lecturing me again.

Janice had sat down beside me on the sofa and listened to my end of the conversation. When I put the phone down, she said, "You're going to go looking for the men who beat you up, aren't you?"

"Yep."

"Gary Cooper lives."

The sharpness in her voice made me look at her. There was a mixture of worry and fear and anger in her eyes. She was trying not to let it out onto the rest of her face.

"What does that mean?" I asked.

"It means you're going to play the hero. You're going to go charging after them and maybe wind up getting hurt even worse."

"You think I should have spilled everything to the cops?"

"You would have been safer that way."

"What about Mandy Traft? Would she have been safer?"

"Last night you wanted to tell the police."

"That was last night."

The exchange was getting heated. I knew even as it was going on that I sounded harsher than I wanted to. It was the confusion that did it. I didn't understand the change in Janice's attitude. I let a second of fairly tense silence go by, then said, "Last night you seemed to think I should try to handle things myself. That's what I'm trying to do. Why does it bother you now? Why not last night?"

She looked at me for a moment, then looked away and said, "That was before I saw you with blood all over your face. Cody, I . . ."

I let my hands hang between my knees. I swallowed and said, "Okay. I think I understand, and I'm sorry. But things are different now for me, too. If I can find those guys, I can maybe find Mandy, too. I feel like I ought to try, anyway."

She stood up, still not looking at me, and went over to the book-shelves. She ran a finger lightly over the spines of the books, pausing when she came to the Westerns. Finally, she said, "I guess Gary Cooper's not so bad after all. I always preferred Bogart myself. He didn't get involved."

"He didn't stick his neck out for nobody, right? How about the endings of *Casablanca* and *To Have and Have Not*?"

She stood still a second longer, then turned around and looked at me and said, "Will you shut up and get to work?" Her lips were turned up in a reluctant smile.

My lips were sore from being punched and that limited the size of the grin I felt. I picked up the phone and started to dial again.

The maid at the Traft house, Alicia, answered with a very hushed and apprehensive, "Hello?"

I said, "This is Cody. Can I talk to Mrs. Traft?"

"Mr. Cody! Have you found Mandy?"

"Not yet, but I may have a lead. Is Mrs. Traft there?"

"Yes, but—we have to get off the phone, Mr. Cody. They said they'd call back!"

"The kidnappers?" I could feel my fingers tightening involuntarily on the phone.

"Yes, they told Mrs. Traft they would call back and tell her what to do with the money."

"All right. When they call, it's very important for Mrs. Traft to pay close attention to everything they say. I'll be there as quick as I can."

I hung up. Janice said, "I'll drive you over there."

"No, I can do it," I said as I stood up.

"In what? Your car isn't here, remember?"

She was right. That was something I had to check on, but I didn't have the time now. Not with things happening so fast. "Could I borrow your—"

"Oh, no. Do you think I'd trust a twelve thousand dollar car to a man with a possible concussion?"

"Come on, Janice—"

"That's exactly what I intend to do." She picked up my jacket and threw it to me. "Why are we wasting time standing around here bickering?"

I slipped the jacket on and shrugged at the same time. "Let's go, then."

I could have done with a shave and a hot shower, and my teeth were crying to be brushed. There was no time, though. I made only one detour on the way out of the apartment.

That was into the bedroom, to open the bottom dresser drawer and take out an oilcloth wrapped bundle. I unwrapped it as Janice stood in the doorway. The .38 went into my pocket, along with a box of shells. Janice didn't say a word, but that look was back in her eyes for a fleeting moment as I stood up.

She drove efficiently and well. The morning wasn't as clear and sunny as I had thought. When we got outside, I could see that gray clouds covered most of the sky, and the sun was only coming through in gaps.

Janice didn't say much as she drove. The only question she asked was, "What are you going to do?"

"That all depends on what the kidnappers tell Mrs. Traft. If they want her to drop the money today, I'll advise her to do exactly what they say. If at all possible, I'll shadow the drop and try to follow whoever picks up the money back to Mandy. It's always possible that they'll follow through and let her go as promised. If it looks like they're not going to, I'll have to try to take her."

When I said that, Janice took her eyes off the road for a second and looked at me, but she didn't make any comment. I suppose she was thinking about heroes again.

There wasn't anything else said until we reached the Traft house. Janice parked in front, and Alicia met us at the door.

"Have they called back?" I asked.

"Not yet." Her face was pale and tight.

"Where's Mrs. Traft?"

"In the study."

I walked through the house quickly, fighting back waves of dizziness. My body would have liked it if I had taken everything a little slower.

Gloria Traft was sitting at the desk in the study, wearing a blue dress and looking calm and composed. It was only when she looked up and I could see the hollow eyes and gaunt cheeks that the strain was revealed. She said in a voice that was full of shock and disbelief, "Mr. Cody . . . they have my daughter."

"I know, Mrs. Traft. I want to help."

"You'll help get her back?"

"I'll try."

She took a deep breath. "Should I call the police?"

"It may be too late for that. We'll have to wait and see what the kidnappers say. Now, tell me what's happened since I left here yesterday morning."

"I—I don't know where to start." Her hands were trembling on the desk.

"Start with the phone call you got in the afternoon. Who was it, and what did they say?"

"It was a man. He asked if I was Mrs. Austin Traft. I said I was, and he said, 'We have your daughter, Mrs. Traft.' Just like that. I asked who he was, but he wouldn't tell me. He said I'd be hearing from them again, that they would give me proof, and I should start getting money together."

"That's all?"

"He hung up then. I didn't know whether to believe him or not. I told myself that it was just some crank or someone trying to get money. I didn't want to believe it might be true. That's why I didn't tell you about it when you were here. Then . . . that package came." A great shudder ran through her.

"About the package," I said hesitantly. "I hate to have to ask you this, but . . . do you think that was Mandy's finger?"

"I don't know." She was fighting back tears. "It looked like it might have been. It's hard to tell."

"And we don't have time for any fingerprinting." I sighed. "What about the phone call today?"

"It was early this morning. It sounded like the same man. He asked if I was convinced. I told him I was."

"Are you?"

"I can't afford not to be. It's too great a risk."

"What happened then?"

"He asked me if I had the money."

"Do you?"

"Not yet. I called our lawyer this morning and told him to start converting the assets held solely in my name into cash until he had a hundred and twenty-five thousand and then to bring it over here. He didn't like it, and he wanted to know what it was for, but I told him to just do it. He will. He's on a sizable retainer."

Some of her spirit seemed to be coming back. That was good. She would need all of it she could get.

"What did you tell the man on the phone?" I asked.

"That the money was on its way. He said he would call back later and tell me what to do with it. He warned me not to call the police or anyone else."

"He didn't offer to let you speak to Mandy?"

"No. Why?"

I brushed past her question with one of my own and was thankful when she didn't press me for an answer. "Could you hear any distinctive background noises while he was talking, anything that might tell you where he was?"

"I think I heard traffic. It sounded like he was outside."

"A phone booth, probably. No way to trace it."

"What do you think we should do now?"

"Well, Mrs. Traft, about all we can do now is wait for the man to call back. When he does, you'll have to listen to him very carefully. Repeat everything he says as he says it, so that I can write it down. There's probably less risk that way than if I try to listen in on an extension. When he's told you what to do with the money, you'll follow his instructions exactly. He'll want you to drop the money somewhere, and I'll be there watching. Whoever picks it up will lead me to Mandy."

"Isn't that taking a chance?"

"Whatever we do will be taking a chance."

She studied my face for a moment, then said, "You don't want to call the police anymore, do you? Alicia said that's the first thing you wanted to do last night."

"The kidnappers will probably want you to make the drop today. The police wouldn't have time to set anything up."

"What happened to your head?"

"A man tried to hire me to not look for Mandy. He gave me five thousand dollars, and his men gave me the rest of it."

"My God! Why?"

"I believe they're probably the kidnappers. They didn't want me nosing around and messing up their plans."

"Do you know who they were?"

"I think the boss might be a man named Waldo Hollis. Does the name mean anything to you?"

She frowned and shook her head. "I'm afraid not. Who is he?"

"He used to be mixed up in organized crime back east. He moved out here when things got too hot for him there. He seems like a man who would be perfectly capable of kidnapping Mandy. I haven't had a chance to check him out yet."

"Oh, Lord." Her fingers curled into fists on the desk. "She has to be all right. She just has to be."

A quiet voice came from the doorway. "Cody."

I turned around and saw Janice standing there. She had waited outside, and I didn't know whether she had been listening to the conversation with Mrs. Traft or not. I looked back at Mrs. Traft and saw that she was staring down at the desk, fists still clenched. I got up and walked over to Janice. She led me out into the hall and said, "Is there anything I can do?"

"Not now. There's nothing any of us can do."

"The maid has been telling me about the phone calls. What do you do next?"

"Wait," I told her, just like I had told Gloria Traft. "We have to wait for the kidnappers to get in touch again."

"Let me know if I can help."

Mrs. Traft called from inside the study. "Mr. Cody." I stepped back into the room.

She said, "I just happened to think. What about Jeff? Yesterday you thought he and Mandy had run away together. That's what you told me when you were here after the man called the first time. I hoped you were right."

"I wish I had been. I don't know where he is, Mrs. Traft. The kidnappers could have taken him, too."

"But his family isn't rich. They couldn't pay much."

"They wouldn't have taken him for ransom."

She thought about what I had said, and her eyes got bigger and more terrified as she understood what I meant.

"It's possible he's not involved at all," I went on. "There's no way of knowing right now. I am fairly sure that he and Mandy did plan to leave together."

Gloria had unclenched her fists and now had her fingers locked together in knots. She said, "I don't understand. Why would they want to run away? Austin and I always liked Jeff. We wouldn't have opposed them if they wanted to get married."

"It could be they didn't want to get married. Maybe they just wanted to live together and they were afraid of how you and your husband would react."

"Well, we wouldn't have liked it, of course, but . . . they wouldn't have had to leave."

"Maybe it was because of Lisa," I said, realizing with a guilty twinge that Lisa was probably still in the hospital this morning and I didn't have the slightest idea how she was doing. "Lisa was in love with Jeff, and she thought Jeff was in love with her. Maybe they felt guilty about cutting her out. I know they tried to keep the romance from her at first." I debated with myself whether to tell Mrs. Traft about what Lisa had done the night before, then decided that she had a right to know. "Lisa tried to commit suicide last night."

"Lisa . . . Suicide? Oh, no. What happened? Is she all right?"

"I think so. She let the house fill up with gas from the stove. I happened to come along and got her out before she had breathed too much of it. She spent the night in the hospital, but the doctors thought she would be all right. She's probably still there."

"My God." Gloria Traft was shaking her head back and forth slowly. "My God," she repeated. "What's happening to everything? Why do all these bad things happen now? They never did before."

I didn't have any answer for that. It seemed to me that bad things had been happening all along. It had just taken them a while to catch up to Mandy Traft and her family and friends.

Mrs. Traft and I sat there in silence for several long minutes. Now that I had thought about it, I would have liked to call the hospital to check on Lisa. I didn't want to tie up the phone, though, and I didn't want to leave and use another phone somewhere else. I would just have to wait on this one, too, like everything else.

Most private detectives, myself included, spend more time waiting than doing anything else. It's the largest part of the job by far, and it's something that can't be avoided. But you never get used to it. Time spent waiting drags just as slowly as it did when you were a kid and couldn't understand why everything adults did seemed to take so long.

There was a digital clock on the desk. The numbers on it flipped around to eleven o'clock, then eleven thirty. I went out and found Janice waiting in an opulently furnished living room that didn't look very lived in. We talked aimlessly for several minutes. I went back to the study and Mrs. Traft.

At eleven forty-five, Alicia came into the room and asked Mrs. Traft if she wanted any lunch. Gloria shook her head numbly and said, "No, thank you, Alicia."

When the maid had gone, Gloria looked at me and said in a voice like crystal shattering, "Dammit, why don't they call? Why don't they call!"

The doorbell rang.

I was the first one into the hall. Gloria and Janice were right behind me. If Gloria wondered who Janice was, she gave no sign of it. I suppose she had too many other things on her mind.

I beat Alicia to the door and waved her away from it. There was a peephole set in the center. I put my eye to it. The lens gave me a fore-shortened view of a gray-haired man in glasses and a conservative suit the same color as his hair. He carried a good-sized briefcase and had "lawyer" written all over him.

"Take a look," I said to Mrs. Traft.

"That's Ross Ansley, our lawyer," she said. "He must have the money. Thank God!"

She swung the door open and said, "Ross! Come in. Do you have the money?"

Ansley stepped inside, adjusted his glasses and looked around. It must have thrown him to see the four of us looking so anxious and appre-hensive. His eyes lingered the longest on me, and there was suspicion in them. He finally cleared his throat and said, "Yes, I have it, Gloria. But I wish you would tell me what this is all about. It's not easy to raise this much cash in one morning."

"I know, Ross, and I really appreciate it." She took the case out of his hand, and I don't think he wanted to let it go.

"You're Cody, aren't you?" he asked me. When I nodded, he said, "I thought I recognized you. Does this have something to do with Aman-da? Has she been located? Is she in trouble?"

I was starting not to like him. He was constantly straightening his al-ready straight tie and brushing his fingers over his carefully styled hair. I would have bet that he was the kind of lawyer who rarely saw the inside of a courtroom. He would be more at home in offices and boardrooms. I was opening my mouth to frame a reply that probably would have been less than polite when I was interrupted.

It was the ringing of the telephone.

Gloria Traft went for it at a run. I came into the study behind her as she said excitedly into the receiver, "Hello? Yes. Yes!"

I had a pen and paper lying ready on the desk.

"Yes, Meandering Road past Camp Carter and the fish hatchery. The Lake Worth Spillway. Yes, I can find it. When? Three o'clock. Yes, just myself, I understand. I've got it. Please don't hurt Mandy! Please—"

She took the phone away from her ear and stared at it with a desperate pleading visible in her eyes. Then she put it down slowly. They had hung up.

Ansley had come into the room, too, and now his shrill voice said, "That was about Amanda, wasn't it? She's been kidnapped! My God, we have to call the police—"

"There isn't time," I cut him off. "The drop is at three this afternoon, isn't it, Mrs. Traft?"

"Yes, that's . . . that's what he said."

"Was it the same man?"

"It sounded like the same one."

"What exactly are you supposed to do?"

"He said to put the money in a plastic garbage bag. Then I'm to follow Meandering Road to where it dead-ends near the Lake Worth Spillway. Do you know where that is, Mr. Cody?"

"Yeah. It's kind of a deserted place during the day. Kids park there a lot at night. What are you supposed to do with the money when you get there?"

"He said there was a concrete retaining wall next to the spillway. I'm supposed to place the bag on it and then leave. He was very specific about coming alone and telling no one about it. I'm not sure I should have even told you, Mr. Cody."

Ansley had been champing at the bit, wanting to get back in the conversation. Now he said, "The thing to do is to tell the police, Gloria. Does Austin know about this?"

"No . . ."

"He's going to have to, you know."

"But why, if we can get Mandy back . . ."

"Because he's my client, too, and I have an obligation to him. While it's true that the assets I converted were held solely in your name, Gloria, that is still a large amount of money. I think I should try to get in touch with Austin as soon as I've called the police."

"The police! You can't call them. The kidnappers said—"

Ansley put his hands on Gloria's shoulders and interrupted her. "If I have knowledge of a crime, Gloria, then it's my duty as an attorney to report it."

Janice Bryant had been standing just inside the study door, listening to the exchange. Now she said, "Cody."

"Yeah?"

"This guy's got a big mouth. Why don't you deck him?"

She did a pretty good Lauren Bacall imitation, even though it sounded a little funny coming from someone like her. I had to agree with what she said, though. I rubbed a hand along my jaw, feeling the rasp of last night's stubble against my palm, and stared at Ansley as I nodded slowly. His eyes widened and he took a step backwards. I curled my mouth in as arrogant a sneer as I could manage with bruised lips and turned away, dismissing him contemptuously. He looked like he would keep his mouth shut.

I dropped the sneer, which had just been for Ansley's benefit anyway, and said to Gloria. "He's right about one thing. Your husband will have to know. There's no way you can keep these things a secret. But we don't have to worry about that right now. Did the man say when Mandy would be returned to you?"

"He said that if I did everything just like he told me, Mandy would be back here before the day was over."

"He didn't let you speak to her?"

"No. Should I do what he said?"

"You should do exactly what he said. I'll be hidden somewhere out of sight, so that I can watch whoever picks up the money and hopefully follow them."

"What then?

"They may lead me to Mandy. If they do, I'll try to rescue both Mandy and the money. If it comes down to it, though, I'll leave the money behind. A girl's life is more important, I think."

She reached out and put a hand on my arm. "You'll be careful, won't you? You won't let them hurt Mandy?"

I looked at her for a long moment before I answered, "No. I won't let them hurt Mandy."

"Thank you, Mr. Cody."

Ansley had the look of a man who wanted to say something again, so I glared at him and went on, "It's three hours until the drop. I'm going to go on out there now and look the place over, find a good place to watch from. You won't see me when you bring the money, but I'll be there."

Gloria sat down at the desk as I turned to go. Janice was waiting for me in the doorway. I took her arm and started out.

Behind us, Ansley had moved in on Gloria and started talking in a fast, smooth voice. I stepped back into the room and said to him,

"Hypothetically speaking, counselor, if you were to try to call the police and I were to put that telephone down your throat, what would happen?"

In a shaky voice, he said, "I'd see that you lost your license."

"It might be worth it."

I hoped that would keep him quiet long enough so that he wouldn't mess things up. Janice walked out of the house beside me.

She went to the driver's side and said, "I'll chauffeur again, right?"

"Only as far as your house."

"What?"

"I'm going to have to borrow your car. Mine's still at Willington's apartment, I hope, but I can't use it. If the kidnappers are the guys from last night, and I think they are, then they know my car. We can't take a chance on them seeing it and getting scared off. I'll have to use yours, since they won't recognize it."

"Why can't I drive you, then?"

"Is it going to sound chauvinistic if I say it's too dangerous for you?"

"Yes."

"Then I won't say it."

She started the car and sent it down the driveway. As she paused before pulling out into the street, she said, "What if I won't let you borrow the car?"

"I guess I'd have to rent one."

"You would, wouldn't you?"

"Yep."

"There he goes with the Gary Cooper imitation again."

She didn't say anything for a few minutes, but I could tell she was headed for her house. Finally, she said, "Are you sure you're doing the right thing by not calling the police?"

"I think so. I really don't think they would have time to set up anything effective. They have too many channels to go through. I'll have a better chance operating by myself."

"You made Mrs. Traft a promise you may not be able to keep."

"I know. I thought of that, too."

Janice pulled up in front of her house a few minutes later and cut the engine off. She turned sideways to face me. "Is there anything else I can do?"

"Pray that things work out all right."

"I will." Her hand came up and touched the bruises on my face. "You be careful, Cody. I like you already, and I think the more I get to know you, the more I like you. I might even love you."

It was close quarters in the little Porsche. Our faces were only about a foot apart. We closed the distance.

The kiss was as warm and sweet as the one the night before, and lasted longer. My arms went around her and drew her nearer to me. When the kiss was over, I put my cheek against hers and whispered into her ear, "I think I might love you, too."

She pulled her head away just enough to be able to look into my eyes. I could see little flecks of gold dancing in the green of her eyes. "Did I hear a but?"

"If Mandy Traft is still alive, I have to do what I can to get her home safely. That's all I can worry about now."

"I understand." She opened the door and slid out. "Take good care of the car. I know you private eyes are hell on automobiles. Try not to wreck it."

"I'll call you when it's over."

She put a hand on my arm and I could feel the strength in her fingers. "Please."

For long minutes after I drove away, I thought about how she looked standing there. I couldn't help but wonder why we had never gotten to know each other before now.

I remembered the first time I had seen her, leading a group of Cub Scouts and two Den Mothers through the Amon Carter Museum, explaining as she went along about the artwork and the artists. The Scouts hadn't paid much attention at first, but they became interested in spite of themselves. The paintings and exhibits have a way of doing that.

There was no question that Janice was a beautiful, intelligent woman, used to the good things in life, while I was a rapidly aging, moderately poor private detective with no bright prospects.

If she wanted to fall in love with me, though, I sure as hell wasn't going to stop her.

I tried to force those thoughts out of my mind. I had told her the truth. Mandy Traft was all I could worry about now.

It didn't take me long to get to Meandering Road, named for the twisting path it takes as it winds its way through west Fort Worth to the back side of Carswell Air Force Base. It ended up in an undeveloped area between Carswell and the southern end of Lake Worth. A state fish hatchery and the privately owned Camp Carter recreation area were the only things in the immediate area. Both of them would be closed up and deserted at this time of year.

Jets roared over every few minutes as I drove along, the big planes taking off and landing at Carswell and the adjacent General Dynamics plant. It had been a while since I had been out there, and I hoped I was going in the right direction.

The Porsche was unfamiliar to me, since I had never driven one of them before, but I got the hang of it fairly quickly. The cut on my forehead had developed a slight throbbing, and a headache had come over me as I drove. It was an annoyance, but there was so much else on my mind that I didn't pay much attention to it.

The road wandered around until I was beginning to wonder if I was lost. The area on my right was heavily wooded. I passed a turnoff with a sign over it that announced Camp Carter. A gate with a chain on it closed off the little drive a few yards off the road.

Just past that, another small road turned off, this time to the left. This was the road to the fish hatchery, and just ahead, I could see part of the massive concrete spillway through the trees.

I slowed down and turned off toward the hatchery. The road curved around a hill and down to the spillway, and a little dirt road angled off into the woods on one side. I turned around and backed the Porsche into it.

When I thought the car would be out of sight, I parked it, got out and walked back toward the spillway to check. The bright red paint still showed up through the trees and brush. Muttering about damn flashy sport cars, I moved it back some more.

This time, when I walked back to the road and turned around to look, I could tell that the Porsche was concealed well enough now, yet was still close enough to get to in a hurry. I started to walk toward the spillway, stepping over empty soft drink cans and beer bottles.

It had been a good ten minutes since I had seen another car. The whole area was quiet and still except for the frequent jets. When there was no noise from them, I could hear the sound of water tumbling over the spillway.

The road ended in a gravel and dirt oval. The spillway was up ahead and to the left, about thirty feet away. The ground rose steeply to the left, with a chain-link fence at the top of the embankment to help keep people away from the lake. I walked up to the edge of the spillway.

There was a concrete wall that ran along the edge of it, just above ground level. Directly in front of me, below the spillway, was a pool that looked deep. Where the overflow from the spillway landed, it churned whitely. Cottonwood trees, bare of their leaves now, surrounded it, and those fallen leaves bobbed and floated on the surface of the pool. To my right, the ground sloped gradually down to the Trinity River bottoms, covered with oak and more cottonwoods. It was a peaceful spot.

I went down the slope to my right and into the trees at the edge of the pond. There was quite a bit of undergrowth and high grass. I found a fairly bushy clump of it with a level, sandy spot behind it. When I sat down and parted the bushes just slightly, I had a view of the wall that would be good enough.

I took my gun and the box of shells out of my pocket. As I loaded it, I wondered how Lisa was doing and if my Ford was still where I had left it. Both things would have been easy enough to check, but I hadn't wanted to take the time. It was important to have the place staked out well before Gloria Traft arrived with the money. I thumbed a bullet into the last chamber of the cylinder.

According to my watch, it was twelve forty-five. The sun had gone behind the clouds, and a damp, chill breeze blew fallen leaves around me. I sat cross-legged with my gun in my lap and waited.

CHAPTER V

IT WAS A long two hours and fifteen minutes. I counted the jets that flew over for a while, and then, a little after two o'clock, had that thrilling activity interrupted by a vanload of kids who drove up to the spillway. There were four of them, two boys and two girls, and they piled out of the van carrying six-packs of beer. None of them looked to be over sixteen, and they had to be cutting school.

I kept an eye on my watch as they sat down, legs dangling over the wall, and started drinking the beer. The boys had their arms around the girls, and there was plenty of giggling and kissing going on. The beer cans went sailing into the pool as they were emptied.

I thought about going up the hill and pretending to be some sort of official, maybe from the water department. I could probably scare them off, but that would reveal my position to anyone who was watching. I just hoped they would be gone by three o'clock.

The hands on my watch moved around to two thirty, then two forty-five. The beer was gone by now, and the two couples were stretched out on the grass. If I had been one to bite my fingernails, I would have been down to the quick by now. There was no way Mrs. Traft could make the drop with them there.

At ten minutes until three, though, one of the boys jumped up and said, "Let's go back to my parents' house. They won't be home for another three hours."

The four of them got back into the van, the girls adjusting their clothes, and I breathed a long sigh of relief as the van went out of sight. I wouldn't have wanted to cut things any closer. The wind made the sweat on my forehead cold.

Gloria Traft was on time. I heard the car coming before I could see it. It was a big cream-colored Lincoln Continental, the current model, of course, and through the windshield, I could see Gloria gripping the steering wheel tightly.

She stopped the car at the end of the road and got out carrying a garbage bag. She was wearing a fur coat and dark glasses. After glancing around for a second, she started walking toward the wall.

She put the bag down carefully when she got there. She hesitated for just a moment, then turned and went back to the car. It took her a few minutes to get the big car turned around and headed back in the other direction.

The drop was made. Now I had to wait and see who picked the money up.

It wasn't a long wait. Only fifteen minutes had passed when I heard another car coming. Just enough time had gone by for the watchers to be sure that Mrs. Traft was gone and wasn't coming back.

The car that came around the curve was one I hadn't seen before, a dark green Oldsmobile. It stopped at the end of the road, too, and the man who got out was familiar. The last time I had seen him, he had been kicking me in the side. My old friend Shelley.

I wanted another crack at him. My head started to hurt worse, and the palms of my hands itched. The time would come, but it would have to wait.

Shelley knelt beside the bag and untwisted the fastener that held it shut. When he opened it and looked inside, I could see a big grin break out on his ugly face. He turned and made a thumbs-up gesture at the car.

There were two other men in the car, one in the back seat, one behind the wheel. The driver would be Frank, the one in the back Waldo Hollis. It looked like I had been right about the identity of the kidnappers. It didn't make me feel a damn bit better.

Shelley closed the bag and picked it up. He went back to the Oldsmobile at a lope. I got up on hands and knees, ready to sprint for Janice's Porsche as soon as they were out of sight.

A new sound froze both Shelly and myself in position. It was coming from down the road. We both stared in that direction. I saw Shelley's lips move, but I was too far away to hear what he said to himself. As for me, I whispered, "Oh, damn."

An old, battered, dark blue Dodge Dart was coming down the road.

It came to a stop behind the Oldsmobile, partially blocking the bigger car. Shelley put his hand inside his coat as Richard Ferrell got out.

I didn't have any trouble hearing what he had to say. His shouts carried over the sound of the water.

"Who the hell are you guys? What's this all about? Where's Mandy?"

Frank opened his door and climbed out from behind the wheel. He kept his gaze on the other side of the car. The rear window on the side slid down and Shelley handed the garbage bag to the man inside.

Frank said, "Look, kid, this don't concern you. Why don't you beat it outta here?"

"If it's about Mandy, it concerns me," Ferrell answered hotly. "I want to know where she is. What was in that bag?"

"We don't know what you're talking about, kid. Now let us out of here."

Ferrell took a step toward them. Frank put his hand inside his jacket.

"You're lying!" Ferrell said. "I've been watching. I saw Mandy's mother put that bag there. What's in it? Is it money?"

"Money?" Shelley said. "Why the hell would anybody leave money layin' around? Nah, it, uh, it's garbage. We're garbage collectors, and it's just trash and stuff."

Ferrell wasn't about to buy that. No one in his right mind would have. A new train of thought seemed to have sprung up in his mind, because his face suddenly got wilder and he cried, "It's money! Ransom money! Oh my God, Mandy's been kidnapped!"

He went into his bull-like charge at Frank. I said, "Dammit!" and started to stand up.

Frank's hand came out holding a revolver. The gun flicked out and snapped against the side of Ferrell's head. He went staggering against the side of the car. Before he could recover, Frank jabbed the barrel into his stomach with brutal force. Ferrell doubled over and started mewling as Shelley came around to that side of the car.

They were about forty feet away from me. Frank and Shelley stood Ferrell up and slammed him against the car again. They weren't looking in my direction, and as far as I could tell, Hollis wasn't either. I started walking toward them. I wanted to cut the distance down as much as I could before they saw me.

Ferrell was moaning and saying, "Oh, God . . . Mandy . . ."

Frank said, "You shouldn't a stuck your nose in, kid. Why'd you come out here, anyway?"

Ferrell gasped and said, "Followed . . . Mr. Cody . . . I knew something was going on . . ."

Damn! I had been paying too much attention to where I was going and not enough to what might have been behind me. I had never noticed him following me, but I might have known he would be hanging around the Traft house and would notice the commotion.

"Cody!" Shelley spat. "That stinkin'—"

I'll never know what he was going to call me. I was only twenty feet away now. I said, "Hold it! Everybody stay still!"

They all jerked their heads around and looked at me. I had my gun up and aimed at them, but they had two weapons, maybe more, to my one. I didn't expect anything but a momentary advantage.

It might have been enough, but I didn't get the chance to find out. Ferrell jerked out of their grip and cried, "Mr. Cody! Where's Mandy?"

Frank's gun was swinging toward me. I shouted at Ferrell, "Get out of there!" but he stood rooted to the spot, right in my way. I tried to sight past him.

The first shot came from inside the car. Hollis fired, and Ferrell grabbed his stomach and screamed, staggering back a step and going to his knees.

Frank and Shelley both fired at me. I held my breath and squeezed off two quick shots in return. They ducked behind the car and kept blasting. Nobody was hit yet except Ferrell. He was still screaming.

There was no cover I could duck behind. The wall and the spillway were the closest things, but to reach them, I would have to turn my back. I couldn't stay where I was, though. Their steady fire would down me for sure.

A bullet whined by my ear and another tugged at my sleeve as I turned. That five-yard run was the longest of my life. I left the wall in a dive, arching out over the pool. I hoped it was as deep as it looked.

It was. I hit the water fairly cleanly and cut into it, the icy shock instantly numbing me. I fought my way back up, grabbed a lungful of air and went under again. In the second I was above the water, I heard Frank and Shelley running toward the wall.

I kept as still as possible and let myself drift. The thick cover of cottonwood leaves on top of the pool and the high, thick grass would help to conceal me.

I was glad that the cold water had made me numb. Otherwise, the running and jumping would have made my wounds from the night before hurt even worse. After a few seconds underwater, though, the cold started to get to me. I started to move myself slowly in what I hoped was the right direction. It was too dark under there to know for sure.

When I finally had to come up for air, I poked just my face above the surface quickly. There were shots being fired, but not at me. Frank and Shelley were plunking randomly at the pool. I was in shallow water off to the side in the shadows, at the edge of a cluster of roots. I kept my head down and pulled myself in among them.

After a minute, I heard Waldo Hollis call out, "You must've gotten him. Come on! Somebody had to hear those shots."

He was right. They had to get out of there before any cops showed up. I rested my head on a root that was half out of the water and tried to suck in as much air as quietly as I could.

There was a big splash, and then a few seconds later, the sound of a car starting. I kept still for a good five minutes after I heard it drive off.

My teeth started chattering as soon as I pulled myself out of the water. I went through the woods and up the slope toward the wall, hugging myself and shivering.

Ferrell's Dodge Dart was still where he had left it. There were tire tracks showing where Frank had maneuvered around it. I saw blood on the ground, but no Ferrell.

That explained the splash. When I stepped onto the wall and looked, he was there, floating face down in the pool. From the size of the puddle of blood on the ground and the way he floated motionless, I knew there was nothing I could do for him. But I slid down the hill, waded out into the water and pulled him up on the bank anyway. His face was twisted in a grimace. I tried not to look at it. There was no pulse that I could find.

I cursed through chattering teeth as I trotted back to Janice's Porsche. I cursed myself, mostly. If I had only noticed Ferrell earlier, I might have shaken him before I ever got there. Then maybe he would still be alive and Hollis and his men would be leading me to Mandy. If she was still alive.

If. Maybe. That didn't do any good. It was too late for speculation, too late for finesse. My gun had gotten lost somewhere in the pond. I'd have to get another one. I was going to find Hollis. Then everyone would have to take their chances.

The Porsche was right where I had left it, undisturbed. I got in, hoping my wet frame wouldn't do too much damage to the upholstery, and turned the engine on. After it had run for a few minutes, I switched the heater on and pushed the thermostat and fan all the way up.

As numb as I was, it took the heater a little while to do me much good. I sat there shivering and let the warm air blow over me. Gradually, I started to thaw. Once some of the chill was out of my bones, a wet clamminess took its place. I had to get home and into some dry clothes.

I drove away, but not easily. I knew Richard Ferrell was back there, and I hated to leave him like that. I thought about all that had happened in the last thirty or so hours and felt a fury growing inside me that was even colder than my skin. Mandy and Jeff and Lisa and Richard . . . There were just too many victims in this case.

By the time I got back to my apartment, I was madder than I was cold. I stripped the wet clothes off as soon as I got in the door and then stood under a hot shower for long minutes. I knew I would have to call Gloria and tell her what had happened, and I felt guilty for putting it off.

When I was dressed again, I sat down on the sofa and pulled the phone over. There was something I had to take care of before I talked to Mrs. Traft. I called the police and told them what they would find at the end of Meandering Road, then hung up before they started asking questions.

I dialed the Traft house and Gloria Traft snatched the phone up on the first ring. "Hello?" she said breathlessly.

I took a deep breath and said, "This is Cody, Mrs. Traft. Have you heard from the kidnappers since the drop?"

"Mr. Cody! Where are you? Did you find Mandy?"

"No. Things didn't work out like I had hoped. The kidnappers picked up the money, but they didn't have Mandy with them. It was the men who beat me up last night, like I thought it would be. Before they could leave with the money, Richard Ferrell came up. He had been following me. There was some shooting. Richard was killed."

There was a second's silence, then she said, "God . . . oh, God . . . That poor boy! What about Mandy? What do we do now?"

"No one's contacted you?"

"No. I've been waiting for a call or something. Anything! I've been worried—"

"Mrs. Traft," I cut in, "I think you should call the police. Tell them everything I've told you. Don't hold anything back. Tell them you think a man named Waldo Hollis is involved with the kidnapping."

"What are you going to do?"

"I'm going to see Hollis. Right now."

I hung up before she could ask anything else.

A check of the phone directory turned up no listing for a Waldo Hollis. I called the police department again and got Franklin on the line. When he answered, I said, "I need Waldo Hollis' address as fast as you can get it."

"What's up?"

"I just need the address."

"You know I could get in trouble for cooperating so freely with you."

"So from now on, you don't know me. Just do this one thing."

"Okay, okay. He lives out by Riverside Drive somewhere. Let me find it."

He put me on hold and came back in a couple of minutes with the address. I copied it down and said, "Thanks," then put the phone down, cutting him off in mid-complaint.

Now I had to find Hollis and his pals and deal with them.

So I called a guy I knew who ran a pawnshop and said, "This is Cody. I need a gun."

IT TOOK A few minutes of talking to convince him that I didn't mean a gun that was hot. I just needed a gun in a hurry. He told me to come over and take my pick.

I put on my only other jacket, the dry one, and headed for the door, pausing momentarily as I thought about Lisa Montgomery. It wouldn't take long to call the hospital and see if she was still there, and if so, how she was doing, but it was time I didn't have. I had to go on the assumption that Mandy Traft was still alive, as unlikely as that was, which meant I had to find Hollis. I took a towel with me to put on the wet seat of the Porsche.

The pawnshop was on Rosedale, so it wasn't too far out of my way as I cut across town to east Fort Worth. It was late enough that traffic was starting to get heavy. Every red light had a long line of cars waiting, and delays put my teeth on edge. Hollis had his money now. He wouldn't waste any time wrapping things up.

I finally got to the pawnshop and found a parking place down the block. The atmosphere inside was typical—stale, dusty and crowded. There was only one other customer, and the guy who ran the place was shooting the breeze with him over a glass case full of small appliances.

He spotted me and called, "Hiya, Cody!" To the customer, he said, "Take your time. I'll be right back with ya."

"Hello, Harry," I said as he came over to me. "I don't have much time. What have you got?"

"Got a beauty just for you, Cody. You like a .38, right? Check this jewel out."

He reached under the counter and pulled out a pistol. It was a .38 a lot like the one I had lost, but newer and in better condition. I took it from him, checked the weight and balance and swung the cylinder open for inspection. It looked like a good gun.

"You gotta aim a little to the left," Harry said, "but it's a damn good little weapon, Cody."

"How much?"

"For you, eighty bucks."

I couldn't stand around haggling. I gave him the money and put the gun in my pocket. My ammo would fit it, so I didn't have to worry about that.

"You got a good buy there," Harry said. "I got it from a guy who used to run a liquor store. Wasted three stick-up artists with it."

Harry went back to shooting the breeze and I went back to the Porsche. Janice had to be wondering where I was and how things had gone. I hoped that when I did have a chance to call her, I would have better news to deliver.

The overcast had gotten thicker. Dusk would come early. Lights had already started to flicker on in homes and outside businesses. I had to look for a few seconds before I located the headlight switch on the Porsche's complex dashboard.

My next stop was downtown. I cruised along Main Street, looking for Hollis' club, the Emporium. When I had spotted the door to it between a pawnshop and an adult movie theater, I angled the Porsche into the first parking place I found.

It looked like a sleazy enough place from the outside, a narrow front with black painted windows and a neon sign that was garish in the late afternoon light. I put my hands in my pockets, wrapping the finger of my right one around the butt of the gun, then pushed through the door.

It was very dim inside, but I knew right away that this wasn't the place where I had been held the night before. The room was too small and the wrong shape. A bar ran the whole length of the right wall, with a small stage set in front of it halfway down. A bored-looking brunette with very few clothes on gyrated tiredly on the stage. The patrons were mostly more interested in their drinks than in the girl.

Finding a vacant stool at the bar wasn't hard. When the bartender, a longhaired kid with glasses, came over to me, I ordered a beer and then said casually, "Waldo around?"

"You mean Mr. Hollis?"

"Yeah."

The kid drew the beer and said, "Are you a friend of his?"

I put a grin on my face and hoped it didn't look as phony as it felt. "Yeah, we're old buddies."

He put the tall glass in front of me. "I didn't know Mr. Hollis' friends came in this dump. He never does." There was defiance in his voice. "He just sends his goons around to pick up the profits."

"Sounds like you don't like your job very much."

"Mister, if you try to get me fired, you'll be doing me the biggest favor of my life."

I said, "Forget it, kid," and dropped a ten on the bar. The beer was untouched, and I left it that way.

He was looking after me strangely when I left, but the ten-spot had disappeared.

The Banjo Room on East Lancaster was Hollis' other club. I stopped at a phone booth and looked up the exact address in the battered directory.

It didn't take too long to get there. I went on down Main and hit Lancaster where it ran under the Overhead Freeway. Traffic was heavy up above, but not too bad down where I was.

The club was in a building by itself, with a giant banjo painted on the side and a big sign proclaiming that there were sensuous nude dancers inside.

They weren't completely nude or very sensuous as far as I was concerned, but that wasn't important. What mattered was that I recognized the place as I stepped inside. I felt a slight kick of nausea as I remembered what had happened to me in the back rooms less than twenty-four hours earlier.

There were quite a few customers. I kept my head down as I went inside, but some of them may have recognized me anyway. It didn't matter. They were the type that minded their own business. Most of the time.

I hadn't gotten a good look at the bartender the night before, so I didn't know if this was the same one or not. I went up to him, keeping my face partially averted and my voice low, and said, "Is Hollis around?"

He was distracted, concentrating on serving drinks, and he snapped, "Ain't seen him."

"He hasn't been around today at all?"

"I told you, I ain't seen him. You deaf?"

One of the men at the bar nudged his neighbor and said drunkenly, "'You deaf?' That's a good one!"

I had been watching the bartender for any signs that might tell me Hollis was really there. So far there had been none. He just seemed like a busy man who was preoccupied with his work.

So was I. And my work was a hell of a lot more serious and deadly than handing out drinks. Suddenly angry, I slipped the gun out of my pocket and pulled the hammer back. When I said, "Are you sure about that?" and the bartender looked up, annoyed, to answer my question, he found himself staring into the barrel less than six inches away. Most of the customers didn't even notice.

The color drained out of his face and he swallowed nervously. In a weak voice, he said, "Oh, damn."

"Do you remember me?"

"Mister, I never seen you before."

"How about Hollis?"

"He ain't been here all day, I promise."

His eyes flicked down toward the bar. There was probably a weapon of some kind down there, and he was itching to get it. But he was too afraid to make his move.

"Forget it," I told him. "While you're at it, forget I was ever here. You can stay alive that way."

More of the patrons had noticed the gun now, and there were beginning to be shouted questions. Somebody cut the jukebox off, dropping silence like a dead weight on the room. I backed toward the door.

No one made a move to stop me. They just stared. But I didn't put the gun up until I was outside and in the Porsche and roaring away.

It hadn't been the smartest stunt I'd ever pulled. The bartender might try to get hold of Hollis now and warn him that a crazy man was gunning for him. I hoped that Hollis was at his home. It would take me only a few minutes to get there.

A few minutes could mean everything in this case, though.

I went on out Lancaster to Riverside Drive. It's an old part of town, with a lot of small businesses and residential areas. There are some nice houses, and the one where Waldo Hollis lived was one of them. It was a frame house, one story, set well back off the street behind a lawn larger than the others in the neighborhood. I drove past it slowly. There was only one light on that I could see. An asphalt driveway led up one side of the lawn and went past the house to a garage in back. The garage was open, and I thought I saw the big Oldsmobile inside. It was too dark to be sure, though.

I parked at the curb down the street, thankful for the darkness that was closing in rapidly. It would make the house easier to approach. Before I left the car, I made sure that each chamber in the gun held a bullet.

I got out, shutting the car door quietly. I tried to look casual as I strolled down the street with my hands in my pockets. I sure as hell didn't feel casual.

There was no visible activity going on at Hollis' house. The light was on in the living room, but the curtains were drawn. I walked past the house, ignoring the walk that led up to the front door.

On the other side of the driveway was a hedge that separated the property from the one next to it. As soon as I passed that hedge, I ducked behind it. I followed it toward the back.

A minute later, I had forced my way through a small gap in the growth and was standing at the side of Hollis' house in the driveway. There was a door at this end of the house, but I wasn't ready to try to get in yet. I walked out to the garage carefully, avoiding clumps of fallen leaves. The Oldsmobile was there, all right, along with the silver-blue Corvette, but they were both locked and empty. There was nothing unusual in the garage, just some tools and junk.

I went back to the house and paused at each window, seeing and hearing nothing. There was no sound of people talking, no television or radio playing. If anyone was here, they were keeping awfully quiet.

Hollis and his men could be gone, cleared out. Even if they thought I was dead, they might be afraid to stay around now that they had the money. If they had flown the coop, that meant the discovery I had been dreading making might be inside the house.

There was no point in postponing it any longer. I went back to the side door and tried the screen. It was unhooked.

My hand was sweating on the grip of the gun. I put my other hand on the doorknob and turned it slowly. It moved easily and the door came open. I hesitated before swinging it back. It was also possible that Hollis and his men had spotted me and were waiting for me.

I pushed the door open. If they were waiting, they would expect me to hang back before coming in, so I followed the door as close as I could, then threw myself to the floor. My bruised ribs twinged when I landed.

There was no sound except the wind blowing through the open door. I kept still for a couple of minutes, then got to my knees. There was enough light coming around a corner for me to tell that I was in a kitchen. I couldn't see anything out of the ordinary.

I got onto my feet. There still hadn't been any noise. I took a slow step toward the lighted living room.

What I found there wasn't what I had expected.

Shelley was the first one I saw. He was on his back just inside the living room. One hand was clutching at his chest, the other was flung out to the side. There was a gun beside him. His face was twisted in a grimace of pain, and the glazed eyes were still open. I could see the red stain through the fingers of the hand on his chest.

I stood absolutely still and looked around the comfortably furnished room. Frank was lying on his face close to the front door. There were two entrance wounds high on his back. I wasn't going to turn him over.

Hollis, at first glance, seemed to be sitting peacefully on the sofa asleep. A second look revealed the lifeless way his arms hung at his side. He had been taken by surprise, too. They all had.

I swallowed. Four deaths in one day. I was shaken all the way through. I had to force my feet to move.

I went over to Hollis. There was a coffee table in front of him. The garbage bag that Gloria Traft had left on the wall was sitting there, open. There was no money inside.

My head was spinning. It was a double-cross, that much was plain. Someone had been in on the kidnapping with Hollis, someone who had decided that the ransom was too good to split.

This room and its grisly contents had nothing more to tell me. I had to check out the rest of the house as quickly as I could. If Mrs. Traft had followed my advice and called the police, they would probably be arriving any minute.

I went through the house in a hurry, calling, "Mandy! Mandy Traft!"

There was no answer. I turned the lights on as I went, using my hand-kerchief as I flipped the switches. I checked all the closets and even under the beds. No Mandy, not even any sign that she had ever been there.

They were holding her somewhere else, then. Either that, or she was in a shallow grave and had been all along. I felt something churning around in my stomach at the thought.

I didn't look at the bodies as I went through the living room on my way out. Hollis and his men were through now. There wouldn't be an-swers coming from them. I had checked for diaries, notes, records, or papers of any kind that might give me a lead, but evidently Hollis didn't bring any work home with him. It could be, too, that the killer had taken everything incriminating along with him, in addition to the money.

I went out the side door again, wiping both sides of the doorknob as I did so. The cops would get around to me sooner or later, but the more time I could stay out of their hands, the better.

I didn't worry about looking casual. Not now. I got back to the car and hurried out of the neighborhood as fast as I could, even though I didn't know where I was going.

There had to be something I could do. I couldn't walk away when Mandy and Jeff were still missing and four people had been killed. The problem was where to start. Franklin might've been able to tell me who some of Hollis' associates were, but word would have gotten around the PD by now about the kidnapping, and he wouldn't answer any ques-tions until he had asked some of his own.

The sight of a phone booth made me stop. I pulled the car up beside it and got out, digging in my pockets for change. It was an old-fashioned glass booth, one of the few left. I closed the door behind me, but cold wind still came in the cracks.

Janice answered on the second ring. I said, "It's me."

"Cody? Thank God! What happened? I was so worried I thought I was going to scream."

"My plan didn't work." The taste of failure was bitter enough; hav-ing to admit it to her only made it worse. "Everything got screwed up. Richard Ferrell, Mandy's ex-boyfriend, followed me and interrupted the kidnappers as they were picking up the money. They killed him."

Janice didn't say anything, but I could still hear her breathing. I went on, "The kidnappers were the ones who worked me over last night. I just came from their place."

"Cody . . . you didn't . . .?"

"Somebody beat me to it. All three of them were dead when I got there. The money was gone and so was Mandy."

"She wasn't there?"

"No sign of her."

"Does Mrs. Traft know?"

"Not about this last. I told her about what happened with the money and about Ferrell. I also told her to call the police. If it's all right with you, I'm going to hang on to your car a little longer."

"What are you going to do?"

"Mrs. Traft probably told the cops my part in this. They'll want to pull me in for questioning, especially when they find those bodies. I still have things to do, and I'd rather do them in a car they can't link up with me."

There was a lot of pain behind my eyes. I closed them and massaged them with my fingertips as Janice asked, "What about you? How are you feeling?"

"I'm all right. It's just that I have to be doing something, something to help."

"Cody," she said, her voice soft yet urgent, "you're blaming yourself, and it's not your fault. You've done everything you could."

"I've done everything I could to mess things up. I told Mrs. Traft to call the cops right at the first, before she even hired me. She would have been better off if she had."

"No one knew Mandy had been kidnapped then."

"Dammit," I said savagely, "I knew later! I should have done something, come up with a better plan. If I wasn't able to do that, I should have kept my hands off. Now at least four people are dead, and one of them was a big innocent kid who didn't do anything but fall in love!"

"Cody," she said, and now her voice was as harsh as mine, "if you think you've screwed things up so bad, why aren't you trying to straighten them out?"

It was a good question, and I didn't have an answer. All I could do was growl, "Blast it! I'll talk to you later."

I hung up and fed more coins to the phone. When the hospital answered, I said, "I'm checking on a patient who was admitted last night. Her name is Lisa Montgomery. Could you tell me how she's doing?"

"Just a moment, sir. I'll check."

I watched the headlights of passing cars as I waited. After a few minutes I heard, "Sir, Ms. Montgomery was released this afternoon. Could I help you with anything else?"

"She was doing all right?"

"Evidently."

"Okay, thanks."

I didn't want to go barging in on Lisa so soon after her experience the night before, but about all I could do now was barge in and ask questions, and Lisa was a place to start.

I headed toward the house near TCU. I felt a burning and stuffiness in my head that told me a cold might be coming on.

There were lights on in the house when I pulled up in front of it. I went up the walk to the porch and knocked on the door.

A few seconds went by. I heard footsteps on the other side, but the door didn't open. Lisa called, "Who is it?" Her voice sounded flat, hollow.

"It's Cody."

I heard her fumbling with the knob, and then the door opened. There was no light in the living room, but the light in the hall was on. It shone behind her, putting her face in shadow. She said, "What is it? Have you found Mandy?"

"Not yet. Some things have come up that no one expected. Could I come in and talk to you for a few minutes?"

"I guess so."

She reached up to unhook the screen. I noticed for the first time how thin her hands were. With long slender fingers. I remembered her telling me that she played the piano. It seemed like a month at least had gone by since then, not a little over thirty hours.

I went in. Lisa crossed the room and sat down at the far end of the sofa. I stood in the middle of the room and looked around as best I could in the dimness. The windows in the living room that I had broken out the night before had been replaced. The only reminder of the episode was a very faint hint of gas, more a memory than an odor, that lingered in the air.

There was enough light coming from the hall that I could tell Lisa was wearing the same bathrobe and a pair of fuzzy slippers. She should have been cute. Instead, her attitude as she sat there with her head down and her hands clasped loosely in her lap, was one of dejection and defeat. I knew that what I had to tell her would only make it worse.

"Lisa," I said. "I've got some news that isn't very good."

She looked up, and her face was more curious than upset. She said, "What is it?"

"Mandy has been kidnapped."

"Kidnapped?" The exclamation seemed to be startled out of her. It was the first spark of life she had shown. "What . . . what happened?"

"There was a ransom note." I thought it would be wise not to mention what else had been in the box. "Mrs. Traft paid the ransom this afternoon. I was there when the kidnappers picked it up. So was Richard Ferrell. He tried to interfere, and they killed him."

"Richard . . .? Dead? Oh, no. That's stupid. There's no reason . . ."

"I know." I sat down on the sofa beside her. "I want to ask you a question, Lisa. Do you know a man named Waldo Hollis?"

"Waldo Hollis? No, I—I never heard of him." She was still upset about Ferrell. "My God, why would anyone kill Richard? He never hurt anybody. He didn't deserve to die."

"He was trying to find out where Mandy was. He was trying to stop Hollis."

"This Hollis, you say he kidnapped Mandy?" She seemed confused, but that was understandable. A lot had been happening.

"Yes."

"Do you know where she is? Why didn't you follow them?"

"I was planning to. Things didn't work out that way, though. But I found Hollis later."

"Was Mandy with him?"

"No. Hollis and his men were dead. The money was gone, and Mandy wasn't there. It looks like Hollis had a partner who double-crossed him."

I saw the shine of tears on her cheeks. I was sitting fairly close to her, but she leaned over and closed the distance. Before I knew it, her head was on my shoulder and she was sobbing into my jacket.

"Why?" she asked in a choking voice. "Why do all these bad things have to happen? We're just normal people. They shouldn't happen to us!"

I hesitated for a second, remembering how Gloria Traft had said just about the same thing a few hours earlier, then went ahead and put an arm around her. I stroked her soft dark hair and said, "I don't know. All I can do is try to make things right."

"When you love somebody, bad things shouldn't happen! Love should be enough to protect you!"

"I know, I know."

She cried for a few minutes. I just kept my mouth shut and held her.

When the tears had dried and she straightened up, sniffling, I said, "Listen, you're important, too. Did the doctors think you would be all right? Do you need somebody to stay with you?"

"No, I . . . I'll be fine. They said I would have a headache for a few days. But I'll be all right. I can take care of myself. I have been for a long time."

"I thought you said you lived with your grandfather."

"He was too busy taking care of the ranch to bother with me too much. It was more of a farm than a ranch, I guess, but Grandfather had a lot of horses, so I always thought of it that way."

I thought it would probably do her some good to talk for a little while. I said, "Tell me what it was like."

"You really want to know?"

"Yes."

"It was good part of the time and bad part of the time, like anywhere else, I guess. I went to high school in Aledo. It was kind of nice going to a real small school and knowing everybody, but it was boring sometimes, too. College is better. There are more people. Mandy was always the only close friend I had, though."

"How about boys?"

She shrugged. "Not really. Not until . . . Jeff."

I could hear sorrow about to break through again, so I said quickly, "Where was the ranch?"

"Out toward Aledo, off Highway 80. You turn off to the left on a dirt road about a mile from the highway."

I knew the area. It was west of town, about halfway between Fort Worth and Weatherford. It was farm and ranch land, and the little community of Aledo owed its existence to being on the rail line.

"I liked living there," Lisa went on, "except that I spent so much time by myself. I didn't have a car. I rode the horses a lot, though. And Mandy came to see me. She liked horseback riding, too. There was a stock tank in the back, and we would ride out there. She dared me to go skinny-dipping in it once."

"Did you?"

"Only when she did first."

Lisa seemed calmer now, more in control of herself. I couldn't blame her for being upset, what with all that had happened. I sensed more strength, more determination in her now.

"You think you'll be okay?" I asked.

She nodded. "All these bad things . . . There's nothing I can do about them now. Are you going to keep looking for Mandy?"

"Yes. I'm almost at a brick wall, but I'm going to keep pounding at it as long as I can. Maybe I'll break through."

I stood up. It was time I got moving again. Lisa stayed on the sofa.

I got out my notebook, and in the light from the hall, wrote down Janice Bryant's name and telephone number. I tore the sheet out and put it on the table.

"That's the number of a friend of mine," I told Lisa. "If you need anything, or if you just need to talk, you call her. I'm sure she won't mind. She's a good person."

"Thank you. But I'll be fine. You don't have to worry about me now, Mr. Cody."

"I'll be seeing you, Lisa."

"Goodbye, Mr. Cody." Her voice was tiny and quiet.

I went back to the Porsche and sat there for a minute, thinking, before I started it up. I hadn't really expected Lisa to know anything about Waldo Hollis. I was still up against that brick wall, running out of punches. I decided it was time to pay another visit to Gloria Traft.

I stopped at a Seven-Eleven before I got to Ridgmar and used the phone to call the Traft house. The maid answered the phone on the second ring.

"Alicia, this is Cody. Don't say my name. Are the cops there?"

She hesitated, then said, "Yes."

"A bunch of them?"

"No."

"Just a couple?"

"Yes."

She was good, knowing right away not to say too much. I asked, "Are they where they can hear you?"

"Yes."

"Does it look like they'll be leaving anytime soon?"

"It's possible."

"Okay, I'll call back every fifteen minutes until they're gone. I'd like to talk to Mrs. Traft, but not with cops around. Make them think this call was just somebody selling something, okay?"

"No, I'm not interested."

"That's good."

"No, we don't need any storm windows," she said and hung up with an abrupt click. I was damn glad there was a good actress in the Traft household.

My stomach made me aware that I hadn't eaten since morning as I waited to call again. I went into the store and bought a soggy ready-made sandwich, a bag of potato chips and a candy bar. I ate the make-shift meal in the car. It landed hard on my empty stomach.

Gloria Traft answered my next call with, "Mr. Cody?" She sounded like she was about to fall apart. I didn't blame her.

"Yeah. Are the police gone?"

"They left a patrolman out front. The detectives are coming back later."

"Okay. I'll come on over and come in from the back. I'd like to talk to you."

"What is it, Mr. Cody? Do you know where Mandy is? Is she still alive?"

"We'll talk when I get there, Mrs. Traft. I'll be there in just a few minutes."

It took me four minutes, to be exact. I circled the block and spotted the patrol car parked in front of the house. I went past it going just under the speed limit and gave it only a casual glance. Using my blinker, I turned right at the next corner.

I took the next right again, bringing me parallel with the street the Traft house faced. The other houses in the neighborhood all had lights on, and I didn't relish the idea of cutting through someone else's property. This was a neighborhood of luxuries and expensive furnishings, and, consequently, a neighborhood of elaborate security systems and guard dogs. If I was lucky, I wouldn't stumble over anything like that.

I didn't. I parked at the curb at what seemed like about the right spot and got out, closing the door as quietly as I could. There were quite a few trees in the backyard of the house I was facing, but I thought I could see the lights of the Traft house through them.

I cut through the property at a cautious trot. I could hear music coming from the house. There was a big garage in back, with room for two cars and a boat. The area next to it was dark and shadowy, so I went through there.

I came to a low redwood fence that was no trouble to climb. When I dropped on the other side, I was in the backyard of the Traft house. It looked like every light in the place was on.

I picked out a French window that led onto a terrace and went to it. It was locked, but the curtains weren't drawn and I could see into the house. I waited until Alicia crossed the hall where I could see her and then rapped lightly on the glass.

Her head snapped around and I could see the tension on her face. She was pale and her mouth was drawn into a thin line. She peered at me through the glass for a second, then realized with a slight start who I was. She hurried over to let me in.

When she had unfastened the window and swung it open, I stepped inside and said, "Where's Mrs. Traft?"

"In the study."

A thought occurred to me. "Alicia, think very hard. Do you know, or did you ever hear anyone mention, a man named Waldo Hollis?"

Deep lines appeared in her forehead as she frowned. "No, I don't think so. And I think I'd remember a name like that."

"He's not very tall, heavy-set, with dark skin and hair." I didn't add that he was also dead.

"No, I don't remember anyone like that."

"Okay. Thanks anyway." I hadn't really expected the question to pay off, but you can never tell.

I took the familiar path to the study and opened the heavy door. Gloria Traft was sitting at the desk, and when she looked up at me, I saw just how much she had aged in the last two days. She looked directly at me and said, "My daughter is dead, Mr. Cody."

I stepped into the study as she continued, "I just know she's dead. It's a feeling."

"Now, there's no way we can know that for sure, Mrs. Traft," I said. "When are the police going to be back?"

"In about an hour, they said when they left. They were going to bring back some equipment to record any phone calls. They thought the kidnappers would call again."

"What did they tell you about me?"

"Just that they wanted to talk to you, to ask you some questions."

"Did they ask *you* any questions?"

"They wanted to know everything that had happened since Mandy disappeared. I told them. Isn't that what I was supposed to do?"

I sat down in a chair, feeling older and wearier than my birth certificate said I had any right to. I answered, "Yes, you did the right thing. I should have insisted you do that right from the first."

"I was the one who was stubborn, Mr. Cody." Her voice took on some strength. Not much, but a little. "If there's any blame, it has to fall on me."

We were both quiet for a moment, then Gloria said, "The police asked me about the same man you did, Mr. Cody. That Waldo Hollis. I told them that all I knew about him was what you had told me."

"Did you tell them I was going to see Hollis tonight?"

"Yes. Was that wrong?"

I shook my head slowly. "No, that's all right. They would have tied me in, anyway. I don't think they'll be able to make anything stick."

"Mr. Cody . . .what are you talking about?"

I rubbed a hand over my face, then said, "I went to Hollis' house tonight, like I said I was going to. I thought maybe Mandy was being held there. Hollis was there, and the two men who worked for him, the ones who beat me up last night. They were all dead. They had been shot, and the money was gone. Mandy wasn't there, and there was no sign she had ever been there."

I wouldn't have thought it possible for Mrs. Traft's face to become tighter, more drawn. It did. She whispered, "My God, what do we do now? What do you think happened?"

"It looks like Hollis had a partner who double-crossed him, shot him and took the money. Whoever he is, he's the only one who knows where Mandy is."

"Can you find him?"

"Mrs. Traft, I don't even know where to start."

I thought for a second, from the look in her eyes, that she was going to scream. Then she shuddered and covered her face with her hands. I felt guilt stabbing through me. I made myself continue, "There's still a chance. The police are in on it now, and they'll know some of the people who might have been working with or for Hollis. They could still find Mandy in time."

I didn't sound convincing, even to myself.

When Mrs. Traft looked at me again, there was a detachment, a faraway look, in her eyes. She said, "You're not married, are you, Mr. Cody?"

I shook my head.

"Then you don't have any children. I always wanted children when I was young. Little girls were still taught to grow up and be mothers then. I married at an early age, and it was a shattering discovery when we found out I couldn't have children. I let it destroy that marriage. Then when I met Austin and when he asked me to marry him, the fact that he had a child already helped me to make up my mind. This way, I could have a family. But there was always something wrong, something between us. It was never anything big, just a constant awareness that Mandy wasn't really my child. Not really."

She didn't seem to want any response from me. I kept my mouth shut and sat quietly.

"Now I feel like she really is my daughter. I know I told people I already thought of her that way. I told you that. But it was never true until now. Now, I feel like . . . like if anything happens to Mandy, it happens to me, too. That's how I know we'll never find her. Not alive. I'm already dead inside."

I stood up, suddenly feeling a desire to be away from this woman, out of this room. Her guilt on top of mine was like thick dust in the air, making it hard to breathe. I turned toward the door, and then she spoke again. There was something in her voice that made me stop and listen. I suppose it was the urgency, the need to share the pain that reached out to me.

"There could have been so many good times. Instead, there were just wasted opportunities. I remember, when Mandy was younger and Austin would be away on business, how she would mope around until he came home. That would have been the perfect time for the two of us to become closer, but she never seemed very interested, so I never made the effort. She would certainly light up when Austin came home, though. One of the best times was when he came home from Hong Kong and brought Muffin with him. He had cabled that he was bringing home a surprise. We met him at the airport, and Mandy wouldn't wait to find out what the surprise was. She made him take it out of his flight bag right there in the terminal. She was only fourteen then, so she could squeal and giggle when she saw the statuette. She thought it was adorable. The carving was exquisite. It was almost too heavy for her, but she took it and hugged it just like you would a real dog. Then she hugged Austin, and they were both laughing . . . I was laughing, too, but not with them. They were too close for that. I was never inside the circle. I was always outside, looking in. After a while, I began to tell myself that was the way I wanted it."

She didn't say anything else. I kept quiet for a minute, then said, "It's not your fault, Gloria. No relationship is perfect. You love Mandy, and that's the most anyone can do."

She looked at me, and there were no tears in her eyes. Only infinite sadness. "It shouldn't hurt so much when you love someone."

There was nothing I could say to that. She was echoing Lisa now, just as Lisa had echoed her.

Something was tugging at my brain, something that I couldn't quite catch hold of. I had the impression that it was something that seemed irrelevant on the surface, and yet I wanted to know.

I stepped over to the bookshelves and stared at the spines of the volumes, trying to let my mind go blank, hoping the elusive something would pop out. It didn't.

I shook my head and turned back to Gloria Traft just as she said, "Muffin was more a part of her life than I was."

"Mrs. Traft," I said, "where is Muffin?"

She looked at me like I had suddenly started speaking in a foreign language. After a moment's hesitation, she said, "Muffin is at Mandy's house. She took it with her when she left here. It was her most precious possession. Why do you ask?"

"It wasn't there. Lisa showed me Mandy's room, and Muffin wasn't there."

"Mandy always kept it on her dresser. It was the closest thing to a good luck charm that she had."

"Was it valuable?"

"Not extremely. Austin paid eight thousand dollars for it."

Eight thousand dollars seemed like a hell of a lot of money to me, but it probably didn't to Gloria Traft. I said, "Someone could have stolen it, I suppose."

"Or Lisa could have done something with it. What does it matter, Mr. Cody?"

She was right. It didn't matter, not now. I didn't know why the thing had gotten in my mind and then demanded to be let out.

I went to the door and said, "Don't give up hope, Mrs. Traft. Like I said, the cops can probably get a line on Hollis' partner."

"What about you? Are you giving up?"

"No. But the cops will be looking for me, too. They know I was at Hollis' house, and they'll want to question me about the murders. I'm probably their number one suspect. Once they get hold of me, I'll be out of circulation for a while."

"What are you going to do until then?"

"Go back to my office and make a few phone calls. I know a few people who might be able to tell me some things about Hollis. That's about all that's left."

As I opened the door, she said, "Good luck, Mr. Cody."

"We all need it, don't we?" I said on my way out.

I SPOTTED THE unmarked car parked in front of my office in time to cruise on past without slowing down too much. I should have known they would be there waiting, in case I showed up. My apartment would be staked out, too. With four murders on their hands, the cops would be very anxious to talk to me.

There was a phone booth outside the supermarket down the street. I went there, parked the car in the store's lot and got out.

I knew at least half a dozen guys who sometimes operated on the shady side of the law. It might take quite a bit of calling around to locate all of them, so I went into the store and turned a five-dollar bill into phone change.

Thirty minutes in the booth turned up nothing. Some of the men I talked to knew Waldo Hollis and some didn't. The ones who did had heard nothing on the grapevine about a kidnapping, and they didn't know anyone who could be considered Hollis' partner. All of them had heard about the killings, and all of them wanted to know if I was the guy who had wasted Hollis. I don't know if any of them believed me when I said no.

I made one last call and listened to the phone ring eight times before it was picked up and an unhappy voice said, "Yeah?"

"I hate to bother you at home," I said, "but you're the last one on my list, Franklin."

"Dammit, Cody, where are you?" His voice was even less happy now.

"Sorry, I can't tell you. I guess I'm pretty hot right now, huh?"

"Scalding. Best thing for you to do would be to turn yourself in."

"Can't do it. Not now, anyway. You think you could help me out on something?"

"I thought you said we didn't know each other anymore."

"I say a lot of things."

"Don't I know it. Cody, did you shoot Waldo Hollis and his goons?"

"Would I tell you if I had?"

"I think you might."

"They were dead when I got there."

"Give me all of it and I might be able to help you."

"I don't have any choice, do I? Hollis and his men and somebody else kidnapped Mandy Traft."

"I know the name. Wasn't it her mother who called us tonight?"

"Yeah. The girl was planning to run away with a boy named Jeff Willington. He's missing, too, and I'm afraid he may have been there when they pulled the snatch."

"They wouldn't have any use for him?"

"None that I know of. I'm afraid it may be too late for him. I think it's just possible Mandy may still be alive, though. The way I read it, Hollis' partner gave him the shaft and took all the money for himself. If Mandy is still alive, he'll know where she is. That's why I need to know who might have been mixed up with Hollis. Did he have any partners in those strip joints of his?"

"Not that we knew about. He could have, though."

"Was Hollis a partner in any other business?"

"Partners in business, partners in crime, huh?"

"I don't have any better ideas right now."

"If he was involved in anything else, it was as a silent partner and I don't know anything about it. You'll have to come up with something else."

"There *isn't* anything else."

I hated to admit it, but it was true. I was at the end of the line. Franklin started making another plea for me to give myself up, but I cut him off with a curt, "Thanks for talking to me," and hung up.

I didn't have anywhere to go now. I stood in the booth and looked out at the nighttime traffic on Camp Bowie. The Kimbell Art Museum was right across the street, and the sight of it reminded me that the Amon Carter was just a block away. If I remembered right, they were open on Tuesday evenings.

I left the Porsche locked up in the parking lot and walked toward the museum. I looked at my watch as I went up the broad steps to the big glass doors. It was just after eight o'clock. The museum would be open for nearly half an hour.

There were just a few people inside, wandering from room to room. I studied the bronze sculptures inside the foyer, both the Remingtons and the ones by other artists. I looked at the Charlie Russell paintings for several minutes before I went on to the next room and began to study the Remingtons there.

As always, the powerful lines and excellent use of color absorbed me. I could feel some of the tension leaving my body. My mind seemed clearer.

I paused in front of the largest painting, the magnificent "A Dash for the Timber." As I studied Remington's depiction of the cowboys' desperate flight for cover from the pursuing Indians, I could almost feel my subconscious going to work, analyzing and categorizing every aspect of the case, trying to find something, anything, that I might have overlooked.

I could almost see the wounded cowboy in the forefront of the group lurch in his saddle. The dust kicked up by the horses' hooves floated in a roiling cloud. I waited and hoped.

Nothing came.

I stood there until time for the museum to close, staring at the painting and standing motionless. I gave a jump when a museum worker came up behind me and said, "We're closing now, sir." From the glance he gave me out of the corner of his eye, I must have looked pretty spooky.

I was the last patron, and as soon as I stepped outside, the doors were locked behind me. I went down the first set of steps and then paused, looking out over Amon Carter Square toward the Kimbell and, beyond that, the lights of downtown Fort Worth.

The night air was cold, and a bright, three-quarter moon was dancing in and out of the clouds. The heavy overcast was breaking up, but I still couldn't see the stars. The lights of the city washed them out. But the moonlight gave the artificial ones some competition, bathing the plaza before me that was surrounded by shrubbery. It was one of my favorite places. If only things had been different . . . but there was no point in that.

"I thought I'd find you here."

I jumped again. People kept coming up behind me. I said, "How did you get here? I've still got your car."

"You mean in all your long detecting career you've never jumped in a cab and said, 'Follow that car!'?"

"Don't push it, Janice," I said, and I must have sounded as harsh as I felt.

She said, "I'm sorry. I didn't mean anything by it. It's just habit."

"It's okay. I shouldn't have been so touchy. It's just that Mrs. Traft trusted me to help her, and now I've run into a dead end. This case has always been just out of my control. I seem to be one step behind."

"You haven't been able to find Mandy?"

"I don't even know where to look anymore."

We were both quiet for a minute, then I said, "How come you came here looking for me?"

"I was worried about you. All of these people are getting killed all of a sudden, and there you are, right in the middle, trying to fix things and make things right. I never thought about you that way before."

"How did you think of me?'

"I thought you were a nice man who was interested in Western Art. As I got to know you better, I realized that you're an intelligent man, too. And a sad one sometimes."

"Everybody is sad part of the time."

"For themselves, maybe. Not for the world. Not everybody."

The waters were getting a little deeper than I liked. I said, "You're wrong about one thing."

"What's that?"

"I'm not right in the middle of this thing. Mandy Traft is."

There was another silence. It was amazing, with Camp Bowie on one side of us and Lancaster on the other, how quiet it was in the square.

Finally, Janice said, "I called your office and your apartment. Your service didn't know where you were. I called the Trafts', and the maid said you had been there and left. I came over here on a hunch."

"You play many hunches?"

"Sometimes."

I had been standing with my hands in my pockets, but now I turned and looked at her and found my arms going out and encircling her. A few minutes went by, and then she said, "Would it help to talk about it?"

"I don't know. I've been over it and over it. I've checked everything I know to check. I've asked everyone about Waldo Hollis, and no one can tell me anything."

She drew her breath in sharply, "Who?"

"Waldo Hollis. The man who kidnapped Mandy."

"You haven't asked everyone."

"What are you talking about?"

"Me. I've heard the name before, and not from you."

I put my hands on her arms, squeezing hard. "Where? From who?"

"I've heard Barney talking to a man named Waldo on the phone several times. I don't imagine it's that common a name. I got the impression he was one of Barney's backers in this new disco."

I remembered what Franklin had said about Hollis being a silent partner in something. A hundred and twenty-five thousand dollars would
pay for a lot of remodeling. The traffic must have gotten heavier, because
there was certainly a roaring in my head.

"You know that for sure?"

"No, I told you, it was just an impression. I don't even know if it's the
same man."

"It's got to be!"

That was all it took. Just a straw to grasp. Suddenly the night didn't
seem so cold and empty anymore. A slim chance is better than none.

Janice was staring at me like I had suddenly started breathing fire. She
said, "Cody, I don't know what you're thinking, but I don't believe that
Barney—"

"Maybe not," I cut in, "but I have to know for sure. I have to check
it out."

"What are you going to do?"

"Do you have a key to the Texas Moon?"

"No. I've only gone there when Barney was there."

"Doesn't matter. Do you know where all the records are kept?"

"What do you mean it doesn't matter? You're talking about Breaking
and Entering!"

"I'm already wanted for suspicion of murder. Do you know where
Wilcox keeps his records?"

"Yes!"

"Tell me where to find them."

"No."

There was no room for argument in her voice, but I tried anyway. "It's
the only chance I've got to find Mandy."

"I know that." She took a deep breath. "I won't tell you where the
files are, but I'll show you."

It was my turn to stare for a second. Then I said, "Come on. Your car's
down the street."

THE TEXAS MOON Disco was dark and quiet. According to Janice, it was
still about two weeks away from opening for business. I parked the
Porsche on a side street a block away.

Janice turned up the collar of her coat as we walked toward the club.
I didn't know if she was cold or nervous or both. I was both.

"There's a door in the back, opening into what used to be the kitchen.

Will that be all right?" she asked.

"It should be. Is it dark back there?"

"I imagine it is, but I don't know for sure. I've never been back there at night, Cody."

Traffic was light on White Settlement Road, which was a good thing. Not as many people would see us skulking around. A drive led around to the back of the building, and we went up it at a fast walk.

It was dark enough in the back. Big trees in the backyard cut down on the light. Janice pointed out the door. I whispered, "Do you know anything about the burglar alarm system?"

"Sorry, Cody. I haven't had anything to do with it yet."

I didn't have a flashlight, so I had to work by feel. I finally found a little plastic box sitting above the door, with insulated wires coming out one side of it and running into the doorframe.

"I don't know how this damn thing works," I mumbled. "Can you put your hands on those files in a hurry?"

"There are too many of them to take with us, Cody. And it'll take a while to go through them all, anyway."

I stepped back from the door and considered it. I tilted my head and looked up. The building had two stories, but I thought I saw a light glint off a window even higher up. "Does this place have an attic?" I asked.

"Yes, it's used for storage. Why?"

"Because I think I see an attic window in a gable up there and I'd be willing to bet that it's not hooked into the security system."

"I wouldn't think so. How in the world would anybody get up there without a ladder?"

She looked at the tree I pointed out, a big thick oak that was growing close to the building. It rose up well above the level of the roof. Janice said, "You're kidding, aren't you?"

"The time for kidding is over." I went to the tree and gauged the distance to the lowest branch. It was within jumping distance.

Janice said, "Cody, don't be crazy," as I jumped and grabbed the branch, chinning myself on it until I could throw a leg over and pull myself up the rest of the way.

"Don't worry. I climbed a lot of trees when I was a little kid."

"You're not a little kid anymore."

She didn't have to remind me. My sore ribs were doing a good enough job of that.

I went from branch to branch up the tree just like I used to when I was eight years old. A little slower, maybe. I had to pick my way carefully, choosing limbs that would support my weight. It wasn't long before I was able to look down on the Texas Moon's roof.

I couldn't see Janice anymore. The shadows near the house were too deep. I paused and studied the roof.

It was only about five feet away. I was sure I could make the jump, but the idea still wasn't too appealing. There was no other way, though. Being above it like I was would help.

I steadied my feet on a thick limb and took a deep breath. Janice must have been able to see me, because I heard a faint, "Oh, no," just before I leaped out.

My feet hit the edge of the roof and then my momentum was carrying me forward. I splayed my fingers out and grabbed desperately at the rough shingles. The pebbled surface gouged at my hands, but I managed to get some purchase and hang on.

I was glad that the slope of the roof wasn't any steeper. I pulled myself up and rolled into a sitting position, catching my breath. The gable with the window in it was about twenty feet away.

It was an old-fashioned window divided into four sections. I crawled over to it. I couldn't see any kind of alarm hooked to it.

I slipped a boot off and wrapped it in my jacket. Two quick raps with the heel knocked one of the small panes out without too much racket. I reached inside and unfastened the catch, then slid the window up. A second later, I had wiggled through it and dropped into the darkness.

Janice had said the room was used for storage. I felt my way around it, bumping my shins several times on unknown objects before I found a door. It was unlocked. There were steps on the other side.

When I had the door closed behind me, I took my lighter out and flipped it on. The glow it gave off let me move a lot faster.

The short flight of stairs led into a hall on the second floor. I went down it quickly, picking up a flashlight from a utility closet on the way.

I was looking for the stairs that led down to the first floor when I felt a funny, instinctive tingling. It was justified a second later by a flurry of quick padding footsteps. I caught my breath and spun around.

The flashlight beam framed a picture that scared at least a year off my life. Racing down the corridor after me was the biggest, blackest dog I had ever seen. Its jaws hung open, revealing rows of sharp white teeth.

I breathed, "Oh, hell!" as it left its feet in a leap. I dropped to one side as fast as I could, and those teeth clamped down on the shoulder of my coat, tearing the fabric but missing my skin. Better that than the intended target, my throat.

The dog's weight staggered me, but I kept my feet. I knew that if I went down it would all be over but the growling. As it snapped at my face again, I swung an elbow that caught the animal in the ribs and knocked it aside momentarily.

So far there had been no noise except my grunting and thrashing. This dog was a killer, capable of handling intruders without making a sound. I swung the heavy flashlight as hard as I could.

It thudded against the dog's shoulder, making it let out a yelp and back off slightly, teeth still bared. It would only be a second before it attacked again.

Out of the corner of my eye, I saw a door that opened off the hall. It was partially open now. I flicked the light in that direction, saw a toilet inside and made a jump for it.

The dog beat me there. Which was exactly what I wanted.

It grabbed at my arm again, but with my other hand I was able to shove it away and into the room. I jerked the door shut, feeling the wood vibrate as the dog hit it from the other side. That didn't bother me now. Big and mean he might be, but I didn't think he could operate a doorknob.

Miraculously, I hadn't lost any blood in the exchange. My coat would never be the same, though. I went back to looking for a way downstairs and found it a few seconds later.

It took me a few minutes to find the switch that cut off the alarm system. When I had it shut down, I hurried to the back door and unlocked it for Janice.

When she was inside, she said, "Are you looking for a partner in the detective business, Cody?"

'I never thought much about it. Why?"

"If you are, count me out. I don't think my nerves could stand it. That was the longest five minutes I've ever spent."

Five minutes? I thought it had been half an hour, at least.

"What happened to your coat?" she asked suddenly, frowning.

"You didn't tell me about the dog."

"Barney's dog? He leaves it here sometimes at night. You mean Punkin did that?"

Punkin? I thought about it for a second and decided it might be better not to say anything.

"Well, come on," Janice said. "I'll show you where Barney keeps his paperwork."

We spent twenty minutes in Wilcox's office, going through his desk and filing cabinets. We both made discoveries at the same time.

"Here," Janice said, handing me a ledger. "Take a look at this."

I shone the flashlight on the figures and the initials written down beside them. It was a listing of money received from and money paid to one W.H.

"It might not mean anything," Janice went on. "It might be someone completely different."

"I don't think so," I said, showing her the photograph I had found tucked into the bottom of a file and probably forgotten. It showed Barney Wilcox and Waldo Hollis grinning at the camera; Hollis had his arms around Wilcox's shoulders. "That's Hollis," I said, pointing him out. I slammed the ledger shut. "That does it!"

"Does what?" Janice asked. "All it might prove is that Barney and Hollis were partners in this club. It doesn't prove that Barney had anything to do with kidnapping Mandy Traft."

"It's all I've got to go on, though. Where does Wilcox live?"

"He has a townhouse on Roaring Springs Road. Mandy isn't there, though."

"How do you know?"

"Because I went to a party Barney had there Sunday night. She wasn't there then. I saw the whole place."

"She could be there now, though. Are you up to some more Breaking and Entering if Wilcox isn't there?"

"We won't have to. I've got a key."

I didn't say anything for a minute. Then, in a quiet voice, "Oh. That's good."

"Cody, wait a minute! Listen to me, please. He gave it to me Sunday night. I . . . I haven't used it yet. And I don't think I ever will."

"Janice . . . I didn't mean . . ."

She dug in her purse and slapped the key in my hand. "Oh, shut up! I didn't mean you couldn't use it."

I turned the key over in my fingers. "Thank you," I said.

We left through the back door.

THE TOWNHOUSE WHERE Barney Wilcox lived was dark, too. I talked Janice into waiting in the car, even though she didn't like it. I put my right hand in my pocket and wrapped the fingers around the grip of the .38 before I slipped the key into the front door.

I swung the door open and stepped inside as fast as I could, shutting it behind me. I didn't want to be silhouetted in the opening.

Nothing happened. I stood with my back against the wall, straining my ears for the slightest sound, for a good three minutes. When there was no response to my entrance in that time, I took the flashlight out of my other pocket and pushed the switch up.

The light slowed me an elegantly furnished living room with modernistic furniture and deep shag carpet and abstract paintings on the wall. The carpet was white, the furniture black, giving the room a decided starkness. I skirted a low coffee table with a thick glass top on my way to the other rooms.

They were more of the same. There was a fashionable sterility about the place that would have made it impossible for me to live there. There was also no sign of Mandy Traft, no sign that she had ever been there.

"No luck?" Janice asked when I climbed back into the Porsche.

"Nothing."

"You tried, Cody. You did your best. Shouldn't we call the police now and tell them about the connection between Barney and Hollis?"

"Are you sure you want to turn your boss in?'

"If he is mixed up in this, you're damned right I want to. And if he's not, there's no real harm done."

"You might lose your job."

"There are other jobs. You may lose your license, too, but that didn't stop you from trying to help Mandy."

"Maybe I could have helped more if I had stayed out of it. Yesterday morning when I first talked to Lisa and saw how cold the trail was—"

Janice glanced over at me when I broke off and saw the look on my face. She said, "Cody, what's wrong?"

I was remembering. I was remembering why Barney Wilcox had looked familiar to me the first time we met. I was remembering a place that had been mentioned more than once that I had failed to check out. I was remembering a jade dog that wasn't where it was supposed to be. And the things I was remembering were starting to form a picture. It was incomplete, but what there was of it was ugly.

"Cody," Janice said, sounding anxious now, "Cody, are you all right?"

"Damn," I said slowly. "Damn-it-all."

Maybe sometimes it's better not to remember.

CHAPTER VI

I EXPLAINED AS much of it as I had figured out to Janice as I drove her home. She didn't want to believe it, and I didn't want to, either, but I had gone too far to walk away from the case now. I had to check this out.

When I stopped in front of her house, I said, "Give me twenty minutes, then call the police. Tell them what I told you, and tell them where I've gone."

"How do you know I won't call them as soon as I get inside?"

"You won't."

"Listen, Cody, you could be completely wrong about this, and even if you're right, you might wind up getting killed. Why should I let you do this?"

"You'd let Gary Cooper do it."

She said, "Damn you," and then she was out of the car and running toward the house. I hit the gas.

It took me about five minutes to get to Interstate 20. Once I was on the freeway, I kept an increasing pressure on the accelerator. The speedometer needle was up to 90 before I had gone a mile.

I was thankful for the Porsche, and that made me wonder briefly if my Ford was still where I had left it the night before. That seemed like ages ago. It didn't really matter, though, not after everything else that had happened.

A sign flashed by telling me that it was twenty miles to Weatherford. I was moving past the other traffic, hoping there were no Highway patrol cars working radar up ahead. Even if there were, I wasn't planning on stopping.

I covered the ten miles or so fast enough to qualify for a dozen speeding tickets. The Aledo exit came up sooner than I had expected, and I had to slam on my brakes to make it.

The narrow farm-to-market road turned south from the highway. I fishtailed onto it, and when I had straightened the car, I sped up again. I had to hold the speed down now to a certain extent, since I didn't know exactly where the next turn was.

Lisa had said it was about a mile off the highway. I slowed down when seven-tenths of a mile had gone past on the odometer. About a hundred and fifty yards further down the road, a small dirt and gravel road turned off to the left. That had to be the one.

I piloted the Porsche onto it, having to slow down considerably now due to the roughness of the road. The night was dark, and the surrounding countryside was dotted here and there with the blue glow of mercury vapor lamps at every farmhouse.

I had gone about a quarter of a mile when I saw a mailbox on a drunkenly leaning post. A dirt lane turned off to the right just past it.

I brought the car to a stop. In the glare of the headlights, I could make out dim letters on the box that spelled out MONTGOMERY.

It was the right place. I turned into the lane. I could see the farmhouse looming up in the darkness and a big barn behind it. There were no lights showing anywhere, and I didn't see any other cars.

The house was ringed by trees. I pulled up in front of it, switched off the lights and cut the engine. It suddenly seemed very quiet.

Now that the headlights were off, the glow from the moon took over and I could see the house even better. It was a square, hulking frame structure with a big front porch and a high, steep roof. I hoped I wouldn't have to climb it.

I got out of the car, carrying the flashlight in one hand and the .38 in the other. There was enough moonlight for me to make my way onto the porch. There were three steps leading up to it, and every one of them squeaked under my weight.

I shone the flashlight on the front door. There was a screen with a wooden door behind it. A dirty window took up most of the top half of it, but it was too smudged for me to see anything through it.

With the hand holding the flashlight, I reached out and tried the screen door. It opened, and I could see the layer of dust that coated it. The knob of the inner door had been shiny brass once, but years of use had dulled it. White paint was flaking off the door in large strips. It looked like the place had been deserted ever since Lisa's grandfather had died and she had moved out.

I tried the knob. It turned a few inches and stopped. The door was locked, but I didn't think I would have to worry about burglar alarms on this one. I took a bead on the lock and slammed a boot heel into it.

The lock gave with a splintering sound and the door popped open. It swung back and hit the inside wall hard enough to rattle the glass. I went through in a rush, flicking the light from side to side.

There was nothing in the room but bare walls and dust. It had been the living room at one time. There was a fireplace on one wall. I shone the light in it, but ancient ashes were all that was there.

There were doors in two walls of the room. I took the one that led into the kitchen first. It was empty, too. The wooden floor and the white porcelain sink that was chipped in places so that you could see the black steel underneath reminded me of my own grandparents' house.

The hall that ran through the middle of the house had an opening from the kitchen as well as from the living room, so I entered it there. There was a bedroom at the back, then a bathroom and then two smaller bedrooms up front. I checked all of them out.

There was an old newspaper in the closet of the back bedroom, and that was it. I used the light to check every possible hiding place, but there was just nothing in the old house. Its outward appearance hadn't lied. It was deserted.

That left the barn. I went back through the kitchen and out onto a small wooden back porch. As I cut across toward the barn, I noticed a crude, handmade swing hanging from the limb of a tree. That brought back memories, too.

Memories weren't important now, though. I was running out of places where I might find Mandy Traft still alive. If the barn was empty, that meant I could start looking for a grave.

The barn's big double doors were closed but not locked. I swung one of them back and stepped inside. As soon as I did, I heard a flurry of tiny scurrying noises, the first sounds I had heard that I hadn't made myself. The mice that inhabit every barn, deserted or not, were running for cover.

I flashed the light around and felt my heart beginning to sink. There were a few bales of dry hay in one corner, and I found a rotten, half-chewed harness in one stall along with a rusty shovel, but that was it. There was no indication that anyone but the mice had been there in recent months.

That left the loft. A built-in wooden ladder led up to it. The wood looked a little rotten. I put my gun back in my pocket, not liking to do it, but I would need a free hand to climb.

I went up the rungs carefully, testing each one before trusting my weight on it. When I got to the top, I hung on with one hand while playing the light around with the other.

There was nothing there but the bare wooden planks.

I put the flashlight down and rubbed my eyes. That was the end of it. The spark of hope that I had had earlier was gone. Either my wild idea had been completely wrong, or Mandy was dead and buried somewhere on the farm. That wasn't much of a choice.

I climbed back down. I didn't feel like covering the whole farm looking for the grave, but something told me that I would have to. My footsteps on the packed earth echoed hollowly in the empty barn.

I picked up the shovel and went out, closing the barn door behind me. As I turned back toward the house, the flashlight beam picked up something I had missed earlier, and suddenly I felt very foolish.

Nearly all of these old farmhouses had a cellar, and this one was no exception. The entrance was at the side of the house. I had overlooked it before, but now I went for it at a run.

I saw the shine of new metal as I got closer, and my pulse quickened. When I got there, I saw that the hasp was held together by a padlock that hadn't been there long. There had to be a reason why someone would lock up this old cellar.

I knew I couldn't break the lock, so I put the point of the shovel under the hasp and threw my weight on it. It took several tries, but finally the nails holding it on gave with a squeal, and the hasp popped loose, torn from the wood.

I dropped the shovel and reached down to open the door. The rusty hinges protested as I lifted it. The light shone down on a short flight of wooden steps.

I paused just for a second, then went down carefully, not wanting any of the steps to break under me. The floor here was packed earth, too, and it only took me a second to reach it.

Empty shelves which had once held jars of jams and jellies and preserves lined the wall in front of me. There was nothing there now.

A rasping breath came from behind me, then a moan. I froze.

I didn't stay that way long. I made myself turn around, shining the light in front of me. The first thing I saw was the cot with its dirty blanket.

Then I saw the pale face above the blanket, eyes closed, and I saw the white bandage above the eyes. I saw the long blond hair, dirty and matted now, that framed the face.

I had found Amanda Traft.

I stood rooted to the spot for a long moment, watching her breathe, before I crossed the small room to kneel beside the cot.

There was dried blood on the bandage. I put a hand on Mandy's cheek and found the skin cold and clammy. She was so pale that the skin stretched over her cheekbones seemed to be almost translucent.

I reached under her jaw line and found the pulse in her throat. It was rapid and not too strong, but it was fairly regular.

I felt an anger rising in me stronger and fiercer than any I had ever felt. I was sure that Mandy had been here in this cold, dank cellar, seriously injured, for nearly a week. It was only luck that had kept her alive this long.

Janice would have called the police by now. They would be here soon, and they could get an ambulance faster than I could. There was nothing I could do for Mandy right now.

I was still left with one problem. Jeff Willington was still missing. As I looked down at Mandy, I suddenly remembered something else Lisa had told me, and I thought I knew where I might find Jeff.

I wrapped the unconscious girl a little better in the blanket. It would probably be better if I didn't try to move her, so I left her there for the moment and climbed the steps out of the cellar.

The shovel was where I had dropped it. I picked it up and headed out past the barn in the moonlight, toward the rear of the property.

I found the stock tank Lisa had mentioned after I had gone about a quarter of a mile. It was on a slight natural slope, and a bulldozer had pushed up the other three walls. An oak tree, bare now of leaves, stood just above it. The water level was low, since the summer had been dry, but there was still a good-sized pond in the middle of the tank. Most of the clouds had blown out, and the moon threw plenty of light on the scene. I felt a cold wind blowing on my face as I stood under the naked branches of the tree.

I walked down into the tank and started making the circuit of it. The ground under my feet that had once been mud had dried to a slightly soft, sandy surface. It wouldn't be hard to dig in it.

I found the spot about halfway around the tank. The soil was softer and darker. It had been turned recently. And after one good rain, the water in the tank would cover it up again.

I put the shovel against the ground and pushed it in with my foot. I dumped the shovelful of dirt downslope, toward the water.

I had been digging for about two minutes and already had a sizable hole, when I heard her say, "You don't have to do that, Mr. Cody."

I dropped the shovel in my surprise. She was standing across the tank from me, under the tree, and I didn't have any idea where she had come from.

"I came to visit. The cab driver thought I was crazy when I told him I lived out here. I made him stop out on the highway and walked the rest of the way."

That explained why I hadn't heard or seen a car, although one could have come up while I was in the cellar with Mandy. Hoping that my voice didn't sound as rattled as I felt, I said, "I'll give you a ride back to town."

She was wearing a coat and jeans. I couldn't see her face very well. She ignored my statement and said, "You don't have to dig them up, Mr. Cody. They're both in there. It's my fault they're there."

"Lisa, you're wrong—"

"No, I'm not. I killed both of them." Her voice was flat and expressionless, sounding nothing like the girl I had talked to the other times. The pressure of keeping it to herself had finally gotten to her. "She stole him from me. Betrayed me. I couldn't stand it when they told me they were leaving together and getting married. I had to get out, I had to get out and cool off. I went out and walked around the campus and when I came back . . . when I came back . . ."—her voice broke for the first time—". . . they were in bed together. They didn't even cover up when I came in. I got so mad . . . so mad. Muffin was right there and so I picked him up and started hitting them with him. He was heavy. I hit Jeff first, and then Mandy started to scream, so I hit her once. And then I hit Jeff again. He had told me once that he loved me, and now I could see that it was all a lie. They must've been laughing at me all along. I kept hitting him until there was blood all over the bed . . ."

She looked up at the sky and then shook her head violently from side to side. "I knew someone would find out!" she cried. "I knew someone would find them. I didn't know what to do!" She went to her knees and began to cry.

"So you called Barney Wilcox because you couldn't think of anyone else to call. You told him you needed help." I was compelled now to have it all out in the open, driven to put it in words. "He came to your place with some other men that you didn't know. He said he would take care of everything, but that they needed some place to take the bodies. That's when you told him about this place."

She nodded wordlessly. I went on. "They took Mandy and Jeff and cleaned the place up and told you everything would be all right. Everything would be all right if you just kept quiet. They even told you what to say if anyone asked you about Mandy."

"Yes!" she screamed. "But I couldn't stand it! I kept seeing their faces and all that blood . . . I wanted to tell somebody. I tried to tell Mrs. Traft, but I just couldn't. And then when you started asking questions . . . Mr. Wilcox threatened me. He told me the police would put me in jail. He or one of the others was always watching me."

"I know. I saw Wilcox talking to you yesterday morning but I never recognized him until later." Nearly too late.

She was still sobbing into her hands. "I don't care now. I don't care what anyone does to me. I wish you'd let me die last night. At least Richard might still be alive. I wish I'd died before any of it happened."

I started around the tank toward her. "Lisa, listen to me," I said urgently. "Wilcox lied to you. Mandy's not—"

"Hold it, Cody."

I stopped in my tracks as another figure appeared under the tree. The kind of authority that was in the voice is usually backed up by a gun. I saw moonlight glinting off the revolver that Wilcox held in his hand.

"Sorry, Cody," he went on. "I don't know how you put everything together, but you're not going to spoil it all now."

He was too far away for me to reach him, and my gun was still in my pocket. My hands were empty. All I could do was keep him talking and hope the cops hurried.

"Now take it easy, Wilcox," I said. "There's no need to go waving guns around."

"The hell there's not. You don't fool me for a second, Cody. And you're not going to talk me out of anything, either."

Lisa had turned slightly and was staring at the dark figure looming above her. She said, "Why did you do it, Mr. Wilcox? Why did you make Mrs. Traft think Mandy was still alive? Was it just for the money?"

I said quickly, before Wilcox could answer, "Mandy is alive, Lisa. She's in the cellar. You didn't kill her."

"Shut up!" Wilcox said savagely. "That doesn't change anything! You're still a murderer, Lisa. You killed Jeff, and I put him in that grave. I've got Muffin, too, and he's got your fingerprints all over him."

Lisa wasn't paying any attention to him. She was saying quietly, "Mandy . . . alive? Alive? I thought she was dead, too."

"That's right, Lisa," I hurried on. "Your friend is still alive. It's not too late for you. There are people who can help you."

"It's too late for both of you," Wilcox said. "For all three of you."

"We're not the only ones who know the story," I told him. "Other people do, too. Janice Bryant does. Didn't you recognize her car when you came up?"

"I thought that looked like Janice's Porsche. That's why I stopped down the road. But it doesn't matter."

I said, "You'll never be able to go back to the Texas Moon, Barney."

"Well, I guess I'll just have to take the money and run, won't I, Cody? After all, I earned it."

"By killing Hollis and his boys."

"By more than that, dammit! I was always the one with the brains when I was in the organization. Waldo always got credit for my ideas. But it was me who kept Mandy Traft alive. Waldo wanted to finish her off right at the first. I was the one who thought of the whole plan when I saw that she was still alive. I was the one who got a doctor for her."

"You mean you're the one who used her, who kept her locked up in a cold damp cellar while she was badly hurt. And you let Lisa go on believing that she had killed her best friend. That's what you mean, isn't it, Wilcox?"

I was shouting now. Lisa was the only one close enough to Wilcox to do anything, and I had to get through to her. She was staring at the moon's reflection in the pond, no longer crying, just staring dully.

Wilcox tried to shout me down, but I overrode him. "Mandy will die if we don't get help for her! She'll die like all the rest! Like Jeff! Like Richard!"

Lisa stood up suddenly, putting her hands in her coat pockets. Wilcox was looking back and forth between us, not sure who to watch. I began edging my hand toward the pocket where my gun was.

"If Mandy's alive," Lisa said in a quiet voice, "I have to help her."

"Forget about her, Lisa," Wilcox grated. "She's not worth it. Remember what she did to you. She doesn't deserve your help. Now why don't you go around there with Cody?"

She took a step toward him. "I'm the one that hurt her. Now I have to help her."

Wilcox swung the gun in her direction. "I mean it! Get over there, Lisa!"

He wasn't watching me now. I slipped my hand in my pocket, barely breathing as I did so, and started to grip the .38.

She took us both by surprise. Her right hand came out of her coat holding something. She said, "I'm sorry," and the something in her hand went off.

The bullet knocked Wilcox back two steps. He sat down suddenly on the slope, clawing at his chest. I started around the tank at a run. Wilcox jerked his gun in my direction and triggered it. I felt a big hand slap at my side and my feet went out from under me.

I landed hard, dropping my gun. Lisa seemed to be in a trance, standing there motionless with the little pistol in her hand. Wilcox was gasping and trying to bring his gun around for a shot at her.

He didn't make it.

Lisa fired twice more, and Wilcox dropped his gun and was still. He didn't make any more noises.

There was a big wet spot on my side that was sending a hot weakness through me. I tried to get to my feet and couldn't manage it.

Lisa turned toward me and said, "Are you all right, Mr. Cody?"

"I . . . will be. Thank you, Lisa. You saved our lives. He would have killed us."

"I know. I don't think you deserve to die, Mr. Cody." She looked toward the hole I had started digging and said, "But maybe I do. I couldn't help Mandy now, anyway."

The wind was so cold and I was so hot, all at the same time. It didn't make sense. I said, "Lisa, don't say that. Don't think—"

"When you told me Richard was dead, I knew it was my fault. Just like Mandy and Jeff. I'm glad Mandy's not dead, but it doesn't change my guilt. I brought the gun for myself, Mr. Cody. I guess you'll have to help Mandy."

She raised the barrel to her head. I struggled to get up again, but I couldn't do it. She was all the way across the pond. It might as well have been a million miles.

The low wail of a siren split the night, and I saw flashing lights out on the highway. I could see Lisa outlined against the moonlit sky with the gun at her head, and then a wave of pain hit me. I slipped down and my eyes closed.

I waited for the crash of a gun that never came. There was a splash, and then I heard sobbing. I opened my eyes. The splash had been the gun going into the pond.

"I couldn't do it," Lisa said.

CHAPTER VII

GLORIA TRAFT WAS standing at the window in the study of her house, looking out at the trees in her big backyard. Wednesday had dawned clear and a little warmer, but the strong wind was still with us, moving the empty branches of the trees and whipping the leaves around in little spirals. I was sitting in front of the desk, wincing every so often as the bullet gash in my side twinged.

"Austin is coming home early, you know," she said. "I don't know if he's more upset about Mandy or about the fact that I didn't let him know sooner. He should be here any time."

That was something I didn't want to hang around for. I already had Mrs. Traft's check in my pocket. I had tried to tell her it was for too much, but she hadn't listened.

I wanted to find out how Mandy was before I left. "Did the doctors know any more this morning?"

Mrs. Traft shook her head. "No, they're still not sure how much damage was done. The concussion was a severe one. She may lose the hand that they cut the finger off of. And she has pneumonia, too. They won't promise us anything, Mr. Cody."

"It's hard to make promises."

I was tired. The night had seemed to go on forever. There had been police and ambulances and endless questions. The ambulances had taken Mandy and Wilcox and me away, and the police had hung onto Lisa. Mandy was in serious condition this morning, while Wilcox was critical and not expected to make it through the day. I was patched up pretty good. I had to tell my story at least a dozen times to the cops who had ridden in the ambulance with me. I was confident I would have to tell it a few dozen times more.

"I still don't understand it," Gloria Traft was saying. "All these bad things have happened to us, and we're not bad people. Mandy is so sick, and Jeff and Richard are dead. I suppose I should hate Lisa, but I don't. I just can't understand why it all happened."

I stood up. "I wish I could tell you the answers. But I don't have any either."

"Maybe it's the wind."

"The wind?"

"Yes, this damned Texas wind. It blows all the time."

I looked past her through the window and saw limbs swaying.

"Nothing has a chance to stay still and grow. The wind blows it away. It blows all the good things away."

I didn't say anything to her as I left. If that's what she wanted to think, I wasn't going to stop her. But I didn't agree with her.

It seemed to me that love had started it, started the chain of events that ended at a lonely stock tank. Love was what had tied together Lisa and Jeff and Mandy and Richard. I thought about the way that love had ended for all of them, and I felt sick. Old and sick.

I let myself out of the house. There were still things to do. The police had towed in my car, and I had to get it out of the pound. Then I could start thinking about trying to save my license.

Mrs. Traft's Texas wind slapped me in the face as I stepped outside. It still had plenty of chill in it. I hunched my shoulders and started walking down the drive.

"Cody."

She was waiting for me with the car, the bright red Porsche that suited her so well. She came into my arms and said, "Is everything all right? I love you, Cody."

That put it in the open, and I knew how Lisa and Mandy and Jeff and Richard must have felt when it first hit them. Compelled and defenseless and very, very vulnerable.

I thought about my theory. Maybe Mrs. Traft and I were both wrong. I hoped so.

With the wind blowing in my face and Janice in my arms, I said, "It'll all be fine. I love you, too."

about the author

James Reasoner has been a professional writer for more than twenty-five years, authoring dozens of novels in a variety of genres and over a hundred short stories. He is best known for the mystery novel TEXAS WIND, which has achieved legendary status as a collectible paperback. For several years early in his career, he wrote the Mike Shayne novellas in *Mike Shayne Mystery Magazine* under the famous pseudonym Brett Halliday. Under his own name in recent years he has written a ten-book series of historical novels set during the Civil War and several historical novels about World War II. He lives in Texas with his wife, award-winning mystery novelist L.J. Washburn.

forthcoming **POINT***BLANK* originals

FAST LANE by Dave Zeltserman
"Johnny Lane—the protagonist from hell--to know him is not to love him. He's that rare blend of greed, gluttony, lust, anger, and psycho-pathic rationalization that in real life would make you want to shoot first and never bother to ask questions. With tremendous skill, Zeltserman lures you to a wild ride on the shoulders of a grizzly. You can't let go."
—Vicki Hendricks, author of Miami Purity and Sky Blues

THE BIG BLIND by Ray Banks
Featuring alcoholic chip-chasing double-glazing salesman Alan Slater. A kncklebuster noir from Manchester UK. Fall 2004.

forthcoming **POINT***BLANK* Readers

JAMES SALLIS
"...fierce and original writer working at full power." **—L.A. Times**
ED GORMAN
"one of the most original voices in today's crime fiction"
—The San Diego Union
DENNIS LYNDS
"a novelist of power and quality" **—Ross Macdonald**

forthcoming **POINT***BLANK* classics

SQUEEZE PLAY by James McKimmey
PAYBACK by Russell James
DAN FORTUNE volume 1 by Michael Collins

for more information please visit us at
www.pointblankpress.com

MYSTERY*FILE *is back.*

From the introductory pages of issue #40,
the first issue to appear in several years:

"A primary focus of Mystery*File is not to be an up-to-date news-
letter for the field, but a place where old and new works co-exist,
where older mysteries can be brought up and discussed as well
as those by the most recent hot authors, and where the careers of
writers can be looked at in perspective. Mystery*File will be for
those fans who love to read and talk about mysteries and series
characters, and those who love to make checklists and those who
love to have them."

Contributors to the first four issues include:

Allen J. Hubin	**Lorraine Gelly**
Bill Crider	**Michelle Zafron**
Marv Lachman	**Dan Stumpf**
Mike Nevins	**Walter Albert**
James Reasoner	**Jon L. Breen**
Richard Moore	**Bob Briney**

and many others.

M*F includes reviews and commentary on all kinds of mysteries, from
cozies (and gothics) to hard-boiled private eyes. Included in issue #42
was an interview with Robert Wade, the surviving half of the Wade
Miller writing combo, with a long perspective on his career.

US subscriptions: three issues for $13.00, available from STEVE
LEWIS, 62 CHESTNUT ROAD, NEWINGTON CT 06111. Overseas
and Canada: Please inquire. www.lewis-books.com/Mfile.htm

Printed in the United Kingdom
by Lightning Source UK Ltd.
107550UKS00001B/136